Joy to the Cats

12 Cats of Christmas Romance - book 2

Karen Drew

K.E. O'Connor Books

JOY TO THE CATS

ISBN: 978-1-915378-22-4

Written by: Karen Drew

Chapter 1

Lucy

My breath plumed out in front of me as ice slowly formed on the outside of my car. I clutched the steering wheel with numb fingers, seconds from driving away. I shouldn't have come here.

My gaze cut around the parking lot of the Forever Paws animal shelter. Why had I thought getting a cat would fix my problems?

I dropped my head back and shut my eyes, that familiar, unwelcome tremor running through me. It was the same every time I left my cozy apartment. I should have learned by now. Staying inside was safer. It was easier. If I didn't face the real world, I may just survive.

There was a tap on the window, and I jumped, my eyes shooting open.

A kind-eyed, middle-aged woman wearing a red sweater with a smiling cat on the front looked in at me and waved.

I cracked the window open an inch. "Can I help you with something?"

"I'm hoping I can help you," she said. "You've been sitting out here for half an hour. You must be frozen. Come inside. We've got free hot chocolate and mince pies for anyone visiting the animals today. It's our way of spreading some festive cheer."

My gaze went to the welcoming glow coming out of the main entrance of Forever Paws. I must have passed this place hundreds of times and had never once stopped. I'd always meant to give them a donation or drop off food for the cats, but I'd always been too busy.

Emily, on the other hand, she was always here. I ran my tongue across my teeth, the tremor inside me building.

"You look frozen to the bone," the woman said. "I'm Mulberry."

"Lucy."

"Welcome, Lucy. I volunteer at the shelter, and I have a feeling you're looking for a perfect ball of fluff to bring into your life."

I nodded slowly. That's exactly what I'd been thinking. I'd come here to find... something? Not just a cat. Some simple joy? A tiny spark of happiness at Christmas? Something I'd be missing the whole year. Something that felt a million miles away.

"I have dozens of cats who'd love to meet you," Mulberry said. "Five minutes of your time, that's all I need. I've sprinkled Christmas magic everywhere. I'm sure we'll find you your perfect furry soulmate."

I glanced away, unwelcome tears springing into my eyes. Emily loved cats. I used to tease her that she'd end up a fur covered spinster with a dozen cats as her companions. She'd simply laugh and tell me how amazing that would be.

"I see there's a big space in your heart that's looking to be filled," Mulberry said.

I slid a glance her way, a spark of irritation firing in my gut. This woman knew nothing about me. She had no right to make assumptions. "I'm just here to look. I'm not taking a cat today. I'm not set up for one."

She smiled, and her dark eyes twinkled. "That's what they always say. But once you enter Forever Paws, magic happens. Especially at Christmas time. And we provide a starter pack of goodies, so you can walk out of those doors with an armful of joy."

A lump lodged in my throat, and I swallowed it down. I needed to find a way to get through this difficult time. Emily would have been thrilled that I was here, offering a home to an unwanted animal. And it was a nice way to remember her. Not that I had any trouble doing that. She never left my thoughts.

"How about you fill in your application to adopt and then we take a walk around?" Mulberry said. "You don't have to commit to anything today."

I pressed a hand against the permanent ache in my chest. I had to do something, or I wouldn't get through this Christmas. "Okay, I'll take a look."

Mulberry clasped her hands together and stepped back from the car. "And I'll thaw you out whilst we're at it. You're not even wearing a jacket. It's been below freezing for several days now. Careful of the ice underfoot when you get out."

I was barely aware of what clothes I'd put on to leave the apartment. I so rarely stepped out of the front door these days. My closet consisted of sweatpants, warm sweaters, and thick socks. I looked down at my mismatching gray pants and brown sweatshirt. At least I wasn't wearing my pajamas. That was a win in my book.

I yanked my keys out of the ignition and stepped out of the car. The icy winter wind cut through my clothes, but I barely noticed. My insides had been frozen for so long that this wasn't a new feeling.

Mulberry pulled open the entrance door to Forever Paws and hurried me through. The warmth inside was like a slap to my numb face, and my chattering teeth slowed.

"Take a seat by our Wall of Joy." Mulberry handed me a clipboard with a form on it and a pen. "You start filling in your information, and I'll get you something warm to drink." She hurried away before I had a chance to protest. I still wasn't certain this was the right thing to do.

I looked around the reception area. Everything was so bright and twinkly, it looked like Christmas had thrown up in here. There were sparkling lights everywhere and a huge tree in one corner with presents underneath it. Christmas tunes played in the background.

I hadn't decorated my apartment this year. It didn't feel right. I couldn't imagine ever wanting to decorate again. There was nothing to celebrate.

I glanced at the wall beside me, which was covered in pictures of smiling, happy people with their cats.

Joy and happiness were still out there for some. They were the lucky ones.

I hunched over the clipboard and scribbled in my contact details and what sort of cat I was looking for. I had no idea. I'd never owned a cat before. Emily had always had cats. She'd grown up with them, and as soon as she'd gotten her own place, she'd welcomed one into her life.

Mulberry returned a few moments later and handed me a steaming mug of hot chocolate with melted marshmallows on top. "You drink that while I look over your application and see who would be a good fit for your lifestyle."

I blew on the hot chocolate and took a sip. It was good, almost as good as Emily made, but she'd add chocolate sprinkles on top of the marshmallows.

Sweat prickled under my armpits. I wasn't ready for this. Today wasn't a good day to leave my apartment. No day was, if I had my way.

"Have you looked at the Wall of Joy?" Mulberry asked.

I glanced at the pictures again. All the happiness radiating from those snapshots only highlighted my empty life. "Sure. They're nice."

Mulberry lifted her head from her examination of my application. She tapped on a picture. "I'm particularly proud of this family. Gremlin was a special case. She was brought in traumatized and in a terrible condition. Her new mom, Rosie, took her on, and their lives were transformed."

I looked at the smiling, dark-eyed woman holding a beautiful dark brown tabby cat. Standing next to the woman was an attractive guy with an equally big smile on his face. "How come their lives changed? It's just a cat."

Mulberry's smile looked like she was indulging a small child. "These cats are special. Animals bring joy into people's lives. Gremlin, Rosie, and Archer were made for each other. In fact, I just got a Christmas card from them. They're so happy and were kind enough to make a donation to Forever Paws. Such wonderful people and an equally wonderful cat."

"Lucky them."

"Now the luck is with you. Or should I say Christmas luck? Although I prefer to think of it as magic," Mulberry said. "You get the opportunity to have your own cat."

I shrugged and drank more hot chocolate. My stomach grumbled, reminding me I hadn't eaten breakfast that day, and it was gone noon.

Mulberry tilted her head, her steady gaze remaining on me. "There's not much in your application about your experience with cats."

"I've been around plenty, but I've never owned an animal," I said.

"We like to think of it as a partnership rather than you being the owner," Mulberry said. "It helps if the relationship is an equal one. Although with cats, you can guarantee they will run rings around you. They remember the days when they were worshipped in ancient Egypt."

The ache I carried with me bloomed in my chest. "I've seen that in action. My best friend, she had this cat who was so snooty. She always got her own way. That cat never compromised."

"And I bet your friend adored her."

My head lowered as more tears appeared. "Yeah, she was crazy about that cat. She'd do anything for her."

"That's what happens when you find the perfect cat to suit your life," Mulberry said. "And I have the ideal one for you. I went for a chat with our current residents while waiting for your marshmallows to melt, and they all agreed my selection was just what you're after."

"Residents? Do you mean the other volunteers?"

"No! The cats, of course. They have all the insider knowledge when it comes to making the perfect match."

This woman was more cat mad than Emily. "I just want..." I had no idea what I wanted. There was a part of me that wanted this pain to go away, but if I wasn't hurting, did that mean I no longer cared about losing Emily? That didn't feel right. She'd been gone a year. That wasn't enough time to get over losing her.

Mulberry took the mug from my hand and set it on the reception desk. "I'm sensing you need a lot of Christmas magic. Let's go make that happen."

I stifled a sigh as I stood. It wasn't magic I needed, it was something I couldn't have. Something that had been taken from me so unfairly.

I gasped as Mulberry wrapped her arms around me. Every nerve in my body froze. It had been so long since I'd been touched by anyone. I'd turned keeping my distance from people into an art form.

She patted me on the back and stepped away, her kind smile making me want to weep.

"What was that for?" I asked.

"Everybody needs a hug now and again. Let me take you to Cat Alley. You can get all the hugs you need there."

I stumbled along behind her, my body shaking. That gentle hug had kept me from tipping over the edge. Sometimes, I'd go days without speaking to people, let alone getting a hug from them. When I did make contact with the outside world, it was always work related and usually done over the phone. Being around this bossy, warm, overly affectionate woman felt weird but also strangely comforting.

She patted my arm as if sensing the battle inside me. "You'll make it."

"Make what?"

"The correct choice when it comes to a cat. Right this way."

I sucked in a breath as we entered Cat Alley. A wonky sign declaring where we were sat at the entrance of the corridor. Christmas stockings were hung on the outside of each of the pens we walked past. I spotted several cats and paused to look at them.

"These aren't for you," Mulberry said. "I have a very special cat in mind. She'll fit right into your life."

I tore my gaze away from a scruffy ginger cat who was washing his ears. "Why do you think she's right for me?"

"She's been with us a long time."

"What's wrong with her? Why has no one else taken her home?"

"This cat hasn't shown any interest in people," Mulberry said. "She's been here almost a year. She was discovered by a passer-by under a bush not too far from the shelter. The cat was just lying there, barely moving. The person who found her figured she'd been injured."

"Was she hurt?"

"No, when our vet checked her over, there was nothing wrong with her. In fact, she was in excellent health."

"What happened to her previous owner? Did she move away and leave the cat behind?"

"No, but it's a sad story. The cat's micro-chipped, and when we scanned her, we discovered where she lived. I contacted the owner several times but got no reply, even after leaving a message. So, I contacted the agent who looks after the apartment building the owner lived in. The cat's owner died. Apparently, it was very sudden."

I blew out a breath. "That is sad."

"Ever since then, this cat has been in mourning."

"Cats mourn?"

"Oh, yes. They're clever. They have sophisticated emotional memories and a strong bonding ability."

"She's grieved all year?" I had more in common with this cat than I'd realized.

"I believe so. She only eats enough to survive, and I've never seen her play with any toys, and she's only a young cat. She's missing her owner. Cats struggle to accept loss."

"How can you be so certain? Maybe the cat is just lazy?"

"This isn't laziness; it's grief. Cats are incredible," Mulberry said. "They remember people they haven't seen for a long time. I get a sense there was a special bond between this cat and her previous owner."

"What's the cat's name?"

"Ah! That's a very special thing, too." Mulberry stopped walking and turned. "She's called Fenella Fancy Pants."

My feet refused to cooperate as my head shot up and I stared at Mulberry. "Say that name again?"

She smiled. "It's an unusual name, but it suits the cat. She's got long—"

"I have to see her right now. Which pen is she in?" My heart raced, and my stomach flipped over. It couldn't be, not after all this time.

"We're right here." Mulberry gestured to the pen she stood by. "This has been Fenella's home for almost a year."

I turned to the pen and clung to the wire mesh, my knees shaky and a riot of tremors running through me. "I don't see the cat."

"We have to go in before she'll make an appearance. Fenella rarely comes out of her bed."

I nodded, resisting the urge to shove past Mulberry to get inside.

"And we need to be quiet," Mulberry said. "She doesn't like loud noises or any sudden movements. This poor little cat is suffering, but I think you're right for her. You can turn her life around and get her to love again."

I nodded so hard my neck protested. "I really need to see her."

"Of course. She refused her breakfast this morning, so we can try again with some food. She usually comes out when she gets hungry enough." Mulberry scooped a bowl off the side and filled it with kibble. "Let's go in and see if she'll greet us." She unlocked the pen and entered.

I dashed in and swayed, overcome with a wave of dizziness. I sank to the floor before I passed out, my gaze glued to the small box at the back of the pen.

"Everything okay?" Mulberry knelt beside me.

"Fine. I just got light-headed for a second. I forgot to eat this morning."

She patted my knee. "You stay there and wait for Fenella to come out."

I nodded, my stomach doing somersaults.

Mulberry held the dish of food in front of the box. "Miss Fenella Fancy Pants, it's time for your breakfast. And I've got someone very special here for you. Your new mom."

I couldn't speak, my mouth dry and my insides churning. My eyes widened as I glimpsed a tiny brown velvet covered nose then a set of dazzling blue eyes, ringed with black.

A gasp shot out of me as I stared at the cat. "It can't be." My words were just a whisper.

"What do you think?" Mulberry looked at me, that same warm, calm smile on her face. "Could this be the cat for you?"

I nodded, too choked with tears to speak. This was Emily's cat. Fenella had disappeared after Emily died.

"What do you think, Fenella? Would you like to go home with Lucy?" Mulberry held out a piece of kibble.

Fenella ate a few bites of food before glancing at me. She blinked slowly three times and sniffed the air. Was that recognition in those pretty blue eyes? It couldn't be, not after all this time.

"That's a promising sign," Mulberry said. "Fenella rarely looks at anyone. I'm taking that as a yes from her."

"Absolutely it's a yes." My words came out on a sigh. "She's coming home with me."

Chapter 2

Kelvin

I yanked more clothes from the closet and stuffed them in the black bags. I deliberately didn't pay attention to the familiar sweaters, most of them with cats on them, the long multi-colored scarves, and the velvet jackets Emily loved. They were of no use to her now. I tied a knot in the top of the bag and opened another one, shaking it out.

"How are you getting on, Kelvin?" Mom appeared in the doorway, dark smudges of tiredness under her eyes. Her hair didn't look brushed, and there were deep lines around the sides of her mouth.

"I just got started on the closet," I said. "Emily had way too many clothes. She probably had an outfit for every day of the year."

The briefest of smiles crossed my mom's face. "She loved to shop. The Goodwill will appreciate these, though."

I blinked away tears and turned back to the closet. It felt so wrong, giving away my sister's things. But the apartment had just been sold, and that meant we needed to remove Emily's belongings.

We'd left it almost a year before putting the place on the market. I wanted to keep it longer, but we couldn't afford the mortgage and the taxes.

Mom walked over and squeezed my arm. "It's not easy."

"That's an understatement," I muttered. "This was her place. She loved this apartment. I told her it was too small, and she'd hate the fact there was no elevator, but she proved me wrong. She'd sit by the window in the living room for..." My words choked, and I couldn't go on. Every time I thought about Emily, a red mist of anger colored my vision.

Mom rested her forehead against my upper arm. She seemed to have shrunk since Emily died. "I know. She struggled to make the mortgage payments some months, but she was determined to be independent. She was so happy here."

I stared out the window, not looking at anything, the haze of Christmas lights in other people's apartment windows barely registering.

"Now, other people can be happy here. The couple buying this apartment seem nice. I wouldn't have sold to anyone I didn't think would love it as much as Emily did."

I nodded, forcing down my anger. Mom wasn't to blame for any of this, but my rage sometimes lashed out at the wrong people when I couldn't keep it under control. "I'll clear the closets then take the stuff over to Goodwill. How's Dad doing?"

Mom's soft sigh revealed everything. "He found some photo albums. He's been looking at those for two hours. I suggested he help clear the food in the cupboards, it's only tins and dried goods in there, but I don't think he heard me. I've left him to it."

Everything felt held together by the most fragile of threads. Mom and Dad seemed more broken every time I saw them, and I didn't know how to make things better. Would there ever be a way through this?

A couple of friends had told me it was time to move on. I'd cut them out of my life the second they'd said that. They had no idea how I felt. How I wanted to rage and beat on everyone. I'd failed Emily. I hadn't been able to keep her safe.

"I need to get on, Mom." I stepped away from her, her shaky sadness sliding over me and making my insides quiver. "The Goodwill will be shut in an hour."

She remained standing beside me for several seconds. "Of course. I'll get back to the kitchen." Her soft footsteps faded away as she left the room.

I swiped my eyes and blinked. If I let the tears fall again, they wouldn't stop. Getting rid of Emily's stuff felt like we were erasing her from existence.

I dropped the bag and glanced at her dressing table. It was scattered with her cosmetics, as if she'd just left the room and would walk back in at any second, apply fresh lipstick, and spritz her perfume around.

I picked up a picture on the side of the dressing table. It showed my beautiful, fair-haired sister with a big goofy smile on her face. Her arms were wrapped around her best friend, Lucy Chambers. They'd been so tight, ever since high school, more like sisters than friends. Lucy was the opposite of Emily, tiny, dark-haired, with big, intense eyes.

Choking down a sob, I set the picture back down and turned it away, so I couldn't feel Emily's eyes on me.

People kept telling me that I was still alive, and I had to live my life. But I didn't feel alive, not since the car crash that stole my sister.

I turned toward the raised voices coming from the kitchen and walked out of the bedroom.

Dad stood with his hands clenched, glaring at Mom.

"We have to let this stuff go," Mom said, her face pale.

"Let's turn down the offer. We can afford the mortgage on this place for another six months." Dad ran a hand through his graying hair.

"Then what? We have to do this all over again?" Mom shook her head. "I can't do that."

"We need more time." Dad looked at me, panic flaring in his eyes. "You understand, son?"

I did, but I also understood that Mom and Dad's savings were running low. They were paying their own mortgage, plus this one, and the property taxes. I helped when I could, but they couldn't afford two sets of bills, not without financially ruining themselves.

Dad sighed and shook his head at me, suggesting his disappointment. "I can pick up some extra shifts. I'm just not ready to let her go."

Mom walked over and wrapped her arms around him. Dad stood there like he was made of stone, the muscles flexing in his jaw. "It's just her things. We'll never forget Emily."

"What if we do?" Dad hung his head. "I've been coming here every week, walking around and checking everything is okay. I'd hate to think of anything bad happening to this place. Emily loved it so much."

"If she could, she'd thank you for doing that, but we have to let this go," Mom said.

His head turned to the stove. "I remember all the terrible meals she cooked for us here."

I snorted a laugh. "Emily never could figure out how to use that oven."

Dad nodded. "I still ate everything she made, even that undercooked cake that made me sick."

Mom pressed her cheek against Dad's chest, and he finally circled her with his arms and held her against him. "It's hard for all of us. But we can do it together."

"I... I still need some time. I'm sorry." Dad stepped out of her arms. He glanced at me, his face full of regret, before he grabbed his keys and walked out the door.

Mom turned, her shoulders slumped and her back hunched. She wrapped her arms around herself and stood there, looking lonely, lost, and broken.

I walked over and hugged her, keeping my tears in check. Everyone was suffering. And this time of year was the worst.

The one-year anniversary of Emily's death had just passed. The date had been like a dagger swipe across my heart. I'd tried to get through the day by burying myself in work then going to the gym and working out until I puked, but it hadn't helped. I'd ended up on my knees next to her gravestone, unable to stop the tears from falling. I hadn't left until the sky was dark and an inch of snow had fallen on top of the headstone.

Emily had loved this time of year. She'd always been Little Miss Christmas. Everywhere I looked, there was a reminder of Emily, from the glittering trees in people's windows to the festive tunes that played endlessly.

I couldn't let my parents know how badly I was suffering. It would hurt them too much, and they were already drowning in their sorrow.

I rested my chin on Mom's head and took in a deep shuddering breath, forcing the feelings down as far as I could get them. "It'll be okay, Mom. Dad will come around. He's always been the logical one. He knows this makes sense."

"We just miss her so much." She pulled back and pressed a damp kiss on my cheek before giving me a watery-eyed smile. "Leave the clothes for now. I've put together a box of things I thought Lucy might like. Mementos of their friendship. Perhaps you could take them to her this evening. I'm sure she'd appreciate them. It's been so long since I've heard from her. I'd like to know how she's doing."

I nodded. I desperately needed a break from this place. The walls seemed to be closing in on me and the air too thin. "Sure. I can do that. Will you be okay on your own?"

"Yes, I could do with some quiet time. I'll do another hour here then head on home." She touched my cheek, a tremble in her fingers. "We don't have to clear everything right away. The sale was only agreed two weeks ago. Maybe we can finish this up after Christmas. Give ourselves a break."

"Whatever you think best, Mom." I took the box she handed me and had to force myself not to run out of the apartment. My throat ached, and my eyes stung as I walked away from Emily's place.

I stepped outside into the frigid, frosty air. Weather forecasters had predicted a snow storm, but so far, we'd only had a couple of inches of snow. It must have passed us by.

I glared at the twinkling Christmas lights in the windows of other people's houses as I walked to my car. No matter how much tinsel or how many sparkling lights I saw, this time of year was bleak, cold, and hopeless. No amount of Christmas cheer would help my frozen heart. I wasn't even sure I had a heart anymore.

I placed the box in the trunk of my car and slammed it shut before settling in the driver's seat.

Whatever I did, it didn't make a difference to how I felt. Emily was gone, killed by a drunk driver last Christmas. I hadn't been there to keep my little sister safe from some selfish idiot.

And that was my job. I was her big brother. I was meant to look out for her. I should have been able to do something, stop it from happening.

I sank back in my seat and closed my eyes. I couldn't let this overwhelm me. I had to be the one to hold things together, or the family would shatter.

Dad had started drinking in the evenings, and Mom usually hid in their bedroom, crying over pictures of Emily. And me, well, I hid in work. It kept me grounded, but it didn't make me happy. Nothing could.

I stared at a sparkling Christmas tree in a large bay window. None of us had done a thing about Christmas. We didn't feel like celebrating.

Emily was gone, and it felt like she'd taken my heart with her. I had an empty hollowness in my chest that was packed full of ice.

I started the engine and pulled away from Emily's apartment. I just needed to keep everything together for a little longer. Maybe things would get better soon.

The trouble was, I didn't know how much more fight I had left in me.

Chapter 3

Fenella

I was curled in the tightest ball I could make, my tail covering my nose and my eyes squeezed shut. I'd gotten used to my small pen at the animal shelter, but it hadn't been home. The people there had been kind, but I'd struggled to care about them. I had no plans to care for another human again.

Now, I was somewhere different, and everything was confusing. I had a strange, new bed, a new place for my food dishes, and a different litter tray, but there was a familiarity in all this newness. Lucy. I remembered her from my time with Emily. I even vaguely remembered visiting here a few times in my pram.

I snuggled down tighter in the back of the closet. I'd been hiding in here ever since Lucy took me from the shelter three days ago.

Lucy had spent a lot of time with Emily before she disappeared. They were always together, often laughing, drinking wine, and watching movies. They'd sit for hours on the couch, chatting and giggling. I'd loved hanging out with them. I'd usually sit on Emily's lap or occasionally snuggle in between them, soaking up their combined warmth. They'd always be tickling my head or stroking my belly and feeding me treats.

I adored our girls' nights in.

Then it had all stopped. I'd heard the humans at the animal shelter say cats don't remember stuff, but I remembered the day Emily went missing as if it had happened yesterday.

I'd been out for my usual walk around the apartment block. Emily let me out and followed me down the stairs before opening the big door out into the huge exciting world. She'd been in a hurry and had a parcel to pick up and gifts to buy. She kissed my head, told me to be careful, and that she'd be back in an hour.

She always came back. She'd often hop into her little red car and zoom away but always returned, usually with a parcel or a bag over her arm. She'd tell me about her adventures at a place called a shopping mall. Apparently, there were lots of different stores where you could buy anything you wanted. She'd usually get me a little treat when she was out as well. Often food. I had a soft spot for chicken.

Emily had gone on her adventure, and I did my circuit around the block, checking the smells, seeing what other cats were around. I'd hung out for a while with my friend, Mr. Nibs. We'd rolled around together a few times, sniffed each other, and investigated the scent left by a new dog.

Then I'd gotten bored and needed a nap. My comfy spot on the couch was waiting for me.

I returned to the main apartment entrance and waited. I looked around but couldn't see Emily's car.

So, I waited and waited some more. It had gotten cold, and snow had fallen. I hated that stuff. It was like rain but colder, and it clung to my fur. I snuggled under a bush. Emily would come back soon. I was certain of it.

The problem was, she didn't. I'd stayed under that bush, getting colder and hungrier.

Finally, someone came out of the main apartment entrance. I raced in and up to the apartment. I scratched at the door for hours, scratched until my paws bled, but Emily never opened the door.

I headed down the stairs again and waited until someone opened the main door before going outside. I started looking for Emily, searching along the roads, trying to pick up the smell of her car. It was a weird, intense mix of fumes, but there were so many similar smells that I soon got turned around.

I started calling, hoping she'd hear me and come pick me up, tell me what a sweet angel I was, then feed me fresh cooked chicken from her hand.

I wanted my Emily back. I loved her. She was the best human in the world. She'd picked me when I was eight weeks old, and I knew she was right for me the second we met. She was so warm and soft and did everything I wanted. The perfect human.

I wasn't certain how long I looked for her, but I'd grown really tired. My tongue felt too big for my mouth, and every step hurt. I'd hidden under a bush and closed my eyes.

The next thing I remembered, someone was looking at me. They grabbed me before I could escape. That was how I found myself at Forever Paws with dozens of other cats.

I tried to let the humans know that I had a home, but they didn't understand. Even when they'd run a beeping thing over my back and said Emily's name several times, they never took me back to her.

A few of the humans said it was so sad that Emily was gone, and she must have been a wonderful person because of what great condition I was in. I knew that. She was mine. I'd only ever pick the best human to be with.

And I didn't understand what they meant by Emily being gone. I knew where she lived. If only they'd take me back to her.

But they never did. I never saw Emily again. But I never forgot her.

I shifted my position, giving a little twitch of my tail.

Being with Lucy was better than the shelter. It was quieter in her apartment, and there were no other cats making noise or causing trouble. But Lucy didn't snuggle me right, and her attempt at grooming me yesterday was a joke. I'd given her a scratch to show my disapproval at her bad technique.

She acted like a robot most of the time, providing me with food, water, changing my litter, and that was it. She was more fun when she was with Emily.

I probably was too. I hadn't wanted to play since Emily vanished.

I flipped open one eye as footsteps padded along the hallway and a door closed. I tried as hard as I could not to move, but every time that door closing sound hit me, I had to know what was going on, especially when it involved the bathroom door.

The bathroom was a place of mystery. Where did all the water come from? I was no fan of water, but it spurted out of the large bowl humans sat on to do their business and out of the faucets. Sometimes, humans filled the enormous bowl and wallowed in it. Emily loved taking baths. Occasionally, when I was feeling brave, I'd perch on the edge and stare at the strange bubbles she'd cover herself in. I tasted them once. Never again.

I uncurled, took a few seconds to have a full body stretch, and hopped out of the closet. I wandered along to the bathroom and stared at the door handle. I used to be able to open Emily's bathroom door. I'd jump, grab the handle, and... yes! It worked here, too.

"Oh! What are you up to?" Lucy was perched on the large bowl in the corner with her pants around her ankles.

I dropped down from the handle and looked around. There was a tower of toilet rolls in one corner. I walked over, hooked one out with my claws, and started to shred it. There was something so comforting about shredding paper. It was the feel of it under my paws. I'd shredded a lot of things at the shelter, including six blankets. Some of the humans said it was a stress response. I wasn't sure what that was, but if it involved shredding toilet rolls, bedding, or newspaper, that worked for me.

Lucy hopped up from the bowl, pulled up her baggy sweatpants, and hit the flush. "What's that toilet roll ever done to you?" She scooped it away from me.

I narrowed my eyes and flattened my ears, alternating my glare from her to the noisy toilet bowl.

Lucy's sigh as she washed her hands suggested she wasn't happy. She'd been doing that a lot since I'd arrived, heaving in a big breath as if she'd forgotten to breathe in a long time then puffing it out and dropping her shoulders.

She couldn't be unhappy with me. I was fabulous. Well, usually. I wasn't my normal self. I hadn't been since I'd lost Emily.

Lucy picked up the pieces of toilet paper I'd shredded and placed them in the trash before sliding to the floor and sitting next to me. She made an attempt to scratch my head, but her nails were different to Emily's, and she didn't dig into my fur as far as I liked.

I lay down next to her, my initial burst of energy gone.

"You're as bad as me," Lucy said. "That's all I want to do as well."

I slid a glance her way. What did she mean? She was already on the floor, just like me.

"Maybe we could curl up together and ignore the rest of the world for fifty years or so."

That worked for me, so long as she was happy curling up in the closet. That's where I planned to spend most of my time.

"I am glad I found you, Fenella. I still can't believe you were at Forever Paws all that time. I called them not long after you went missing and asked if they had you. We must have just missed each other. I'm sorry. I should have kept on looking. I wasn't myself after the car crash." Her fingers brushed across my fur. "Do you remember Emily?"

I shuffled my butt until it was on the floor mat. Of course, I remembered her.

"I hope Emily's happy that we found each other," Lucy said. "I'll try to make you happy. It could be a bit hit and miss. You're my first cat."

I lifted my head at the sound of Emily's name. Did Lucy know where Emily was? Had she sent her a message about me? They always texted each other, sending jokes and silly pictures. I often featured in the pictures Emily sent.

Lucy's eyes glazed over as she gently stroked my back. "I'm sorry I didn't find you earlier. Things have been a bit... difficult around here. I don't get out much, anymore. I don't know if you remember, but I used to spend most of my spare time at your place with Emily."

I twitched my nose. I remembered. I was there as well. Emily said I was a full member of the 'girls' night in' gang.

"Since she's been gone, I haven't had anywhere else to go. I haven't wanted to go anywhere." Lucy heaved out another one of those big sighs. "It's not so bad here. I hope you'll get used to it."

I settled my chin back on my paws and let out my own sigh, getting an unwelcome hit from the bleach bottle in the corner of the room. Lucy was talking about Emily, but it didn't seem like she was going to take me to her. What was wrong with these humans? Why couldn't they figure out that I had to be with Emily? It wasn't complicated. We belonged to each other. She was my human, and I was her cat.

We fit together like chicken and beef in a rich meat gravy.

A knock sounded on the main door of the apartment.

Lucy's forehead wrinkled, and she pulled herself to her feet. "I'm not expecting any deliveries today." She padded out of the bathroom.

After a few seconds, I heaved myself up and followed her. The funny gasp and the way Lucy stepped back as she pulled open the door had me speeding up.

I did my own snort-gasp as I stared up at someone who'd been in my life as long as Emily and Lucy. It was Emily's brother, Kelvin.

I skipped on my paws and flipped my tail. He must know where Emily is.

I was so close to being reunited with her. I could just feel it. Any second now, I'd be back with Emily, exactly where I belonged.

Chapter 4

♥

Lucy

I peered up at Kelvin, the surprise at seeing him after all this time making me shiver. "Hi! What are you doing here?"

He stood in front of me, dressed in old jeans and a faded sweater with a hole in the arm. His intense blue eyes reminded me so sharply of Emily that I had to look away for a second. I needed to hold it together. This wasn't the first time I'd seen Kelvin since Emily had died, but it had been a while.

"Hey! Mom thought you might want these." He thrust a box at me.

"What's in it?" I stared at the box.

"We're clearing Emily's apartment. It's some of her stuff."

The words were like a stab to my heart. "You're getting rid of her apartment?"

The way his eyes narrowed suggested he wasn't happy about it. "We've got no choice. Mom and Dad can't keep up the repayments on two places. Do you want the box or not?"

I grabbed it and clutched it to my chest like it was a life raft in a stormy sea. "Of course. Are you... okay?" It was such a lame question. It was easy to see that Kelvin was anything but okay. Beneath his eyes sat weeks of tiredness, and his broad shoulders were slumped as if something heavy pushed down on him. I knew exactly how that felt.

He scrubbed a hand down his face. "I'm managing. How about you?"

"Well, you know. Life happens."

A thin smile crossed his face. "It sure does. Sorry to disturb you." His gaze drifted to the floor, and his head jerked back a fraction. "That looks just like Emily's old cat."

"Oh! It is." I turned to see Fenella sitting observing Kelvin. "I found her a few days ago."

He kneeled on the floor, holding his hand out. "Are you sure? I mean, she's been gone a while."

"As long as Emily," I said. "The shelter checked her chip when they took her in. It's definitely her. I was as surprised as you when I saw her."

A soft laugh slid out of Kelvin. It curled around me like a comforting wave of warmth. I hadn't heard laughter in a long time.

He held his hand out, and Fenella sniffed it. "Do you think she remembers me?" he asked.

I tilted my head as I studied their interaction. "It's hard to tell. She didn't seem scared of me when we met again, and she's certainly interested in you. I've had her three days, so we're still figuring things out." I lifted a hand, meaning to rest it on his shoulder, but paused. This was Kelvin. He'd been in and out of my life the whole time I'd been friends with Emily. And the way my heart flip-flopped in my chest reminded me that I'd always had a crush on him.

"She looks thin." He ran a hand down her spine. "Are you feeding her right?"

"Of course. She's just not eating much. The volunteer at the shelter said she didn't show much interest in food."

"Emily used to feed her by hand."

"I remember. That cat ate better than Emily ever did."

Fenella definitely seemed interested in Kelvin as she leaned against his hand. Seeing him was doing her good. Maybe it would do me good, too.

"Come in. You can get to know Fenella again."

Kelvin stood, his gaze shifting along the corridor, before he nodded. "Sure. Why not? There's no other place I need to be." He stepped over the threshold.

I tugged at the edge of my frayed sweater. When was the last time I'd brushed my hair? I wasn't sure how much of a mess I looked, but on a scale of one to ten, I'd put myself as a high eight. Oh well, he'd seen me looking worse than this. Kelvin had collected Emily and me the first time we'd had too much to drink. I'd ended up puking most of the night. He'd teased me about it for weeks.

And he'd seen me when I got the flu so bad I couldn't even keep down water. I had to look better than that. I shrugged. Why should I care if I looked a mess?

I glanced at Kelvin as he walked into the living room. He was as gorgeous as ever, despite how tired he appeared. Those sharp blue eyes, the messy dark blond hair, and those muscles he got through his work as a landscape gardener were just as I remembered. He'd always done strange things to my insides. Gotten me all flustered and tongue tied.

Kelvin moved a pile of papers off the couch. He set them on the table and looked around.

I did the same, trying to see the place through his eyes. It was a mess. I'd always lived in a kind of messy chaos, but at least it had been clean. I couldn't remember the last time I'd vacuumed. Now I had Fenella, that would have to change, or I'd be overrun with furballs.

"You want a coffee?" I asked.

"That would be good," he said. "I still can't believe you found Emily's cat. Do they know what happened to her?"

"They took her in not long after... after Emily went." I hunted around for two clean mugs as I waited for the coffee to brew. "It was kind of weird. When I went to Forever Paws, I wasn't sure what I was doing. I met this volunteer, Mulberry. She was a bit pushy but told me she had the perfect cat for me. It was as if she knew we had a connection. She led me straight to Fenella's pen, and that was it. I had to bring her home."

Kelvin stroked Fenella, who sat by his feet, her gaze on him. "Maybe this is Emily's doing. She's looking down on you and figured you'd be the best one to take care of Fenella."

The lump that formed in my throat felt hard and jagged. No matter how many times I swallowed, it didn't disappear.

I filled a glass with water and drank until I was able to talk. "I'd like to think that was true." I poured the coffee and walked over to the couch, setting the mugs down on the table, before sitting next to Kelvin.

He nodded a thanks as he picked up his coffee and took a drink. "That's just what I needed. I've been over at Emily's apartment all day with Mom and Dad. There's so much stuff to sort through. Emily was a secret hoarder."

My gut twisted like a broken slinky. "You're braver than me. I don't think I could go back there. There must be so many memories."

"Tell me about it. Dad's a wreck, and Mom's just about holding on by the tips of her fingers."

"How about you?" I asked.

He lifted one shoulder. "As you said, life happens. You have to do these things, no matter how terrible they make you feel. We're donating most of Emily's clothing and furniture to charities. I'd think she'd approve of that."

"She definitely would." I rested my hand on the top of the box I'd set on the floor. I so badly wanted to look inside, but I also knew what a mess I'd turn into when I saw her things.

"If you don't want anything in the box, you just have to say," Kelvin said. "I've got a trip to make to the Goodwill. I'll probably go tomorrow with Emily's clothes and anything else I can fit in the car."

"I'm sure I'll want it all," I said. "It's just that it's… well, they're Emily's things."

"Yeah." That one word held so much pain that my heart thudded in sympathy. We'd both lost someone we loved.

I set my mug down and flipped open the box lid. I didn't look as I put my hand inside and pulled out the first item. It was a picture of the two of us at graduation. That had been an amazing day. We'd been deliriously happy with our whole future in front of us.

"You two were such geeks," Kelvin said softly, his gaze on the picture. "I couldn't have been prouder of her that day, even though I never told her. She worked hard to graduate."

"Emily was so excited when she landed her first conservation job," I said. "The money was terrible, but the joy on her face when she got that offer, you couldn't beat it."

"That was Emily. She always planned to save the world, one injured animal at a time." He reached down and petted Fenella.

I pulled out several scarves, smiling as I ran the soft fabric through my fingers. Emily had always had a thing about scarves. She'd probably owned a hundred but had a dozen favorites, most of which I'd bought for her.

Fenella chirruped and trotted over to the box. She placed her paws on my knee and sniffed at the scarves I held before snagging one between her paws.

"Careful with that," I said.

Fenella flipped onto her side and rolled on the scarf until she was tangled in it.

"Do you think she can smell Emily on the scarf?" Kelvin asked. "Animals have a much better sense of smell than we do."

I stared at Fenella, amazed to see her so animated. "She must. After all this time, she can still remember Emily."

The faintest of purrs drifted up as Fenella continued to roll around on the scarf, flipping from side to side.

I gently placed another scarf next to her, and she grabbed it and started to knead it.

Tears clogged my throat. This was positive. I wanted Fenella to be happy. I needed to make sure she had the best life. It wouldn't be the life she'd had with Emily, but if I could keep this little cat happy, I'd be doing something Emily would have wanted.

I took out a couple more photos from the box and set them on the table.

"You must have a lot of great memories about Emily," Kelvin said.

"Yeah. I'm always thinking about her."

"She was so proud of you."

I turned toward him. "What was she proud of?"

"She was always talking about you. It used to bug me. It was always Lucy did this amazing thing today, or Lucy aced another test, or Lucy got a merit award. She'd tell me you were the sister she'd wished she'd had, instead of an annoying big brother." Kelvin shook his head, a faint smile on his face.

"She was only teasing. She adored you, even though your over-protectiveness used to drive her mad."

"I needed to protect her, especially from the guys she dated. She had lousy taste in men."

I chuckled and nodded. "She did have a way of picking idiots."

"I soon scared them away." His smile grew bigger. "Emily would brag about you setting up your own company. She'd say you were the smartest person she knew."

"Emily was clever," I said, "and relentless. She followed her dream. Most people are too scared to do that for fear they'll fail."

"She was that, all right. That was another thing that used to bug me. She got an idea in her head and wouldn't let it drop."

"I loved that about her."

"I didn't love her attempts to get me into green smoothies. She used to make me a gross pond water surprise every morning and tell me it was good for me."

"It showed she cared."

"It showed she was pig-headed."

I nodded. "Also true."

"Are you still running your own business?" Kelvin glanced at the messy desk in one corner of the room. There were a dozen designs of book covers pinned to the wall.

"Sure. I work from home. I've got a lot going on right now."

"You're closing over Christmas?"

I licked my lips. "Probably not. It's a quiet time, so I can get a lot done."

"You're not seeing your family?"

"I'll call them on the day, but I can't handle the long flight." Mom and Dad vacationed in Florida to keep warm, and I was a snow lover through and through. The thought of a hot sun blazing down at me over Christmas didn't seem right.

"You'll be on your own?"

I pulled my shoulders back. "Not now I have Fenella."

Kelvin's silence suggested he didn't approve. "Are they yours?" He nodded at the designs over my desk.

"That's right. My favorites. I get commissioned to design fiction covers, a few non-fiction as well, but they're not so exciting."

"Emily used to say you were building your own empire."

"This doesn't exactly look like an empire." The dusty surfaces and dirty dishes in the sink suggested a completely different story.

Kelvin squeezed my knee. I jerked away as if he'd fired a bullet through my thigh.

"She'd want you to be happy." His voice was so soft I could barely hear him.

"I'll get there," I said. "I just need some time."

"That's what I keep telling myself. I'll get there. It'll get better. Yet, I wake up every morning and have her at the front of my thoughts." His chin dropped to his chest. "I don't want that to change. The day I wake up and don't think about Emily, it means I'm forgetting her. I can't ever do that."

That same hard jagged ball lodged in my throat again, threatening to choke me. He could have been voicing my own thoughts.

His hand settled on my knee again, and this time, I didn't jump. I placed my hand over his. "Every day, it still hurts. I wake up and think it was a nightmare, and I'll get a text from Emily telling me what movie marathon we're having this weekend and to bring the ice cream. Then the day starts, the message never comes, and I remember this is real. This is happening, and I have to deal with it. We all do."

"And how are you dealing with it?" His fingers flexed underneath mine.

I lifted one of the pictures of Emily and me in a small silver photo frame and ran my fingers over it. "I tell myself that, if I make it through to the end of the hour, I can go back to bed. It feels safe under the duvet. That usually works, and I don't notice until I've tipped over into the next hour and can play the game all over again. Other times, it doesn't help. One of the privileges of being your own boss is that, if you're having a lousy day, you can just quit. Turn your back on everything and try again tomorrow."

"I've reversed that strategy. I've taken on more jobs than I can handle, so I can't think straight. It helps keep me steady. When you've got people on the phone all the time and deadlines hammering toward you like an out-of-control freight train, it makes you focus. At least for a while."

I slumped back on the couch, the exhaustion shoving at me like a callused, cold hand.

"You know, if you ever want to talk about what happened to Emily..." Kelvin's voice faded to nothing.

"I don't. I mean, not yet. My mom keeps suggesting counseling. She told me I was stuck the last time we spoke on the phone and that it's not healthy to live in the past."

"Hmmm, I've heard the same thing once or twice."

"So, I organized my own kind of talking therapy." I'd never told anyone about this.

"How does that work?"

"I joined a group of volunteers who give talks in the community. They're all people who've lost loved ones."

He stared at me. "You talk to strangers about Emily's crash?"

"The first time I did, I almost ran off. It was so difficult. But people were so kind. Sometimes, they need to hear a hard truth before they change."

He swiped a hand down his face. "I couldn't do that. I'd get too angry."

"You don't mind that I'm speaking about Emily?"

"No! Not for a second. It's great, especially if it helps you."

"I've only done a few talks. I thought it would get easier, but the reverse seems to be happening. If anything, I feel like I'm regressing."

Kelvin hummed under his breath and nudged me with his elbow. "Take my number, just in case you want to talk to anyone else. About anything."

I passed him my phone to key in the details. Maybe I would want to talk to him someday.

"Mom often asks about you. She'd love to see you if you ever feel like it. It's no surprise she misses you. You were over at our house most nights when we were kids."

I choked down a dozen emotions that crawled up my throat. I missed Emily's family, too. I loved my parents, but they'd always been at work when I was growing up, so I'd hung out at Emily's most afternoons after school. Her mom was so sweet and gentle, and her dad told the worst jokes. He was always trying to make us laugh. I loved them just like they were my real family.

After Emily had died, I'd cut them out of my life. I hadn't seen her parents since the funeral and had only bumped into Kelvin a few times when I'd dashed out because I'd forgotten coffee or toilet paper. Seeing them again would be a painful reminder of everything I'd lost. Not just Emily, but her family's warm, loving acceptance.

I couldn't see them. It would bring up too many memories. My life was better this way. Maybe not better, but easier and definitely safer. I could handle being on my own. I had my work, and now, I had Fenella. There was no way I was letting anybody else in. I couldn't handle it if they left me, just like Emily had.

I didn't realize my eyes had closed until Fenella chirruped. I looked up to see her trotting out of the living room with one of Emily scarves in her mouth.

"That cat loved my sister," Kelvin said. "I guess some things never change, no matter how much time passes."

I forced myself to sit up straight. My head was so heavy that I wanted to curl up on the couch and close my eyes again. "At least someone's happier now. Thanks for bringing over Emily's things."

He finished his coffee and stood. "You're welcome. And the offer stands. Any time you want to come by Mom and Dad's, they'd welcome you with open arms."

I could only nod and fake a smile. The idea of going over there, being engulfed by the warm, welcoming embrace of Emily's family, seared into me like a hot poker. I couldn't do it. I'd stay here, where there was no risk of getting hurt and losing something I loved.

I walked to the door with Kelvin and pulled it open.

He turned, bent as if to kiss my cheek, but then stepped away. "See you around?"

I lifted a hand. "Sure. It was good to see you." I closed the door and leaned against it.

The ever-present pain that sat just above my rib cage felt a little less spiky. It had been good to talk about Emily and great to see Kelvin, even though it was a painful reminder of the past.

If I could work up the courage, maybe take a shower and wear clean clothes the next time, we could do it again. But I wasn't getting attached. Not ever. That rule was in place for an excellent reason. I only had one heart, and it had already been shattered. What was left needed protecting, or I wouldn't survive.

Chapter 5

Kelvin

Maybe I could hit the flimsy partition wall that separated the living room and kitchen. Slam right through it with my fist. I'd probably break a bone, but it would stop me from laying into the new owners of Emily's apartment.

The last forty-five minutes had been torture as I'd walked around with Jen and Clive Bush, and they'd talked about the changes they wanted to make to the apartment. It felt so wrong. My nerves arched and sparked, warning me that something terrible was happening, and I had to stop it.

A throbbing headache pounded behind my eyes, and my gut churned with an intense sickness I wasn't sure I'd be able to control for much longer. This was Emily's home. Nothing should change. It had to stay just as it was.

"If we take down this wall, we can have a wonderful kitchen diner," Clive said. "Do you know if this is a partition wall?" He tapped his knuckles on the wall I'd been considering punching.

I dowsed the rage inside me in a way Superman would be proud of, before striding over to the wall. "It'll come down. But if you do that, you'll lose the character of the place. It should stay."

Clive glanced at his wife. "We like open plan. Jen's a great cook, and I don't want her trapped in the kitchen when I'm hanging out in the living room on my own."

Jen wrapped an arm around Clive's waist. "It's a perfect idea. We'll get some builders around to quote for the job. Shall we take another look at the kitchen before we go?"

I gritted my teeth. "Take your time." I shouldn't blame these people for wanting to make changes and design their version of perfect. I was the one with the issue.

It felt like, every day, a piece of Emily was disappearing. Her things had been taken out of this apartment bit by bit, then the sold sign went up outside. It would all be changed once Jen and Clive ripped the guts out of it. If I could get into this place after they moved in, all evidence of Emily would be erased. That punched into my gut like a prize fighter on a mission to win a heavyweight championship belt.

If I took out some of my savings, I could pay the mortgage on this place. Just keep it for a bit longer. Keep Emily for longer.

I left Jen and Clive to explore the kitchen and see what they wanted to ruin in there. I walked to the window and stared at the heavy snow that had fallen overnight. There'd already been problems on the roads, and although this one had been cleared, it needed another snowplow to come by soon, or it would be impassable, especially with the hill toward the end.

My phone rang. I pulled it out of my pocket, a bolt of surprise hitting me. "Lucy?" I hadn't expected her to take me up on my offer to talk. From the stubborn set of her jaw when I'd suggested it, it seemed like the last thing she'd want to do. "Everything good with you?"

"No. Everything is terrible. Fenella's missing."

I stepped away from the window. "What happened?"

"She got out of the apartment. Snuck right past my legs when I was taking in some groceries. She ran out the door and along the road. I followed her but lost sight of her. Emily never let her out when it snowed."

"She won't have gone far. Fenella must be familiar with your place by now. She's been there a week. Wait at the apartment. She could be making her way back to you as we speak. I'll come help you look for her. I'll be there in ten minutes."

We said a quick goodbye, and I strode into the kitchen. "Sorry, folks, I need to cut this viewing short."

"We need to measure up for the new units in the kitchen," Clive said.

"You'll have to do it another time. There's a family emergency I need to deal with." They didn't need to know this was about my sister's cat. After all, she'd always called Fenella her baby.

"We can always come back another time," Jen said. "And I want to make it home before the snowstorm gets any worse."

"Good thinking." I hustled them out the door before locking it behind me and racing down the stairs.

A biting, icy wind slapped me in the face as I dashed to my car. I slid into the seat, turned over the ignition, and whacked the heater on full blast. I was just giving the engine a few seconds to warm, when I spotted a small animal stalking across the snow toward Emily's apartment.

All I could see at first were a few splodges of brown, then my eyes widened. "Are you kidding me?" Emily's old cat had her ears flat and her head down as she headed straight for the apartment.

I killed the engine and leaped out of the car. I hurried along behind Fenella, still not believing what I was seeing.

The cat turned, narrowed her blue eyes at me, and raced to the main entrance of the apartment block.

"Slow down. I'm not going to hurt you. You remember me. It's Kelvin." By the time I'd reached the door, Fenella was scratching to get in.

I opened the door, and she raced in and hurled herself up the stairs.

I shook my head. After all this time, this little cat remembered this had once been home. My heart did a sad little throb. "Sorry, kitty. You're too late. This place isn't for you anymore."

I pulled out my phone and called Lucy. "Hey! Something amazing's just happened. Fenella's shown up at Emily's apartment."

"What? Are you sure it's her?"

"It's definitely her. She knew exactly where she wanted to go. Raced up the stairs and to the apartment like a heat seeking missile."

"That's incredible. Fenella must have remembered how to get back home."

"I can leave her here overnight if you don't want to come out in the bad weather. I'll put down something for her to sleep on and a box for her toilet. I may even be able to find something she can eat."

"No, I'll come get her. She can't get used to being there. It won't be fair on her when I take her away."

"The roads are bad. You should stay inside."

"I've driven in bad weather plenty of times. I know how to look after myself. I'll see you soon."

Before I could change her mind, the call disconnected. I frowned at the heavy snowfall outside. "Don't you dare hurt Lucy."

I walked along behind Fenella as she trotted through the apartment, her tail up. She meowed a few times and looked around.

"You sure are a clever cat. You must have walked over two miles to get here and crossed several busy roads. I figured you'd have zero road sense, since Emily usually took you out in one of those embarrassing cat prams."

Fenella ignored me as she dashed around the apartment. She meowed some more before heading toward Emily's old bedroom.

"Ah, I know what you're looking for. Sorry, kitty. Emily's not here anymore. I wish she was. Probably more than you."

Fenella continued to walk around, checking in every room and insisting every cupboard and closet was opened so she could look inside.

Her persistent search for someone she'd never find lodged like a knife in my gut. This animal had no clue what was going on. At least I understood what had happened to Emily, even though it was brutally unfair.

Fenella circuited the apartment five times before there was a knock on the door.

I pulled it open to discover Lucy, her short dark hair plastered against her head, and her round cheeks flushed pink. "Hi. Where is she?"

"In here. She's fine. Getting her bearings. And... I think she's looking for Emily."

Lucy's eyes widened before she blinked several times. "Of course, she is. I didn't even think about that, but it now makes sense why she ran. She wanted to come home."

"How did Fenella know the way here?" I took her damp jacket.

Lucy headed into the apartment. "Emily used to bring Lucy over to my place sometimes. Maybe she remembered the route. Is that possible? It's been a year."

"It looks very possible to me." I pointed at Fenella, who sat in the middle of the almost empty living room, her ears up as she stared at Lucy before looking away. If a cat could look deflated, she did.

A series of emotions crossed Lucy's face so fast I didn't catch them all, but there was sadness shining in her beautiful eyes.

"It must be weird for you to be back here," I said.

"Super weird," she said. "But it feels… different. Most of Emily's things are gone. It doesn't seem like the same place." Lucy ran her foot over the indentations where the couch used to sit. "We had some great times here. It wasn't that we did anything special; it was just fun hanging out with Emily."

"She was great at getting people to feel comfortable around her," I said. "And she had such a soft heart. I used to worry people would take advantage of that."

"I was exactly the same, always telling her to be careful. She was always looking out for other people."

"That was my sister. Heart of gold." A stab of hot pain lanced my chest. "It's always the good ones who get taken way too young."

Lucy nodded but didn't say anything.

"Do you want to take a look around while you're here?" I asked.

Her hand went to her chest before she shook her head. "No, I've seen enough of this place. It's just bricks and mortar. What made it so special was the person who lived here." She bit her lip. "Sorry, that was thoughtless. I know you and your family don't want to let this place go."

I was quiet as I rolled her words around my head. "Actually, that makes a whole lot of sense. This is just an apartment. It's not Emily. Maybe it is time to let this place go. In fact, the buyers were here when you called. I had to get rid of them."

"Oh! I hope I didn't cause any problems," Lucy said. "I panicked when Fenella ran. I knew you'd understand how important she is."

"You're fine. The buyers are sold on this place. I don't think anything will put them off. And they have big plans for it. They want to knock down that wall, fit a new bathroom, and probably update the kitchen."

"Those were the exact plans Emily had for the apartment." Lucy smiled and shook her head. "She said she wanted an open-plan kitchen diner in here. She felt shut away in the tiny kitchen."

"Huh! You don't say? That's exactly what the new people want to do." Maybe their ideas weren't so terrible.

"Emily even dragged me kitchen unit shopping for a whole day one weekend, so she could pick the perfect units. She had some poor guy create a 3D design in-store, so she could see what it would look like."

"How'd she plan on paying for this work? Her job wasn't much more than minimum wage. She was always the dreamer." I turned away and stared out of the dark window, barely seeing the heavy snow cascading from the sky. I missed my sister so much. Missed her easy contentment. Missed how she followed her heart before anything else.

And even though I'd considered her a pain when she'd hung around me when we were kids, I'd loved having the role of her big brother. That was until I'd failed her.

A gentle squeeze on my arm had me turning, and I had to blink to clear my tear-hazed vision.

Lucy stood there, a solid, living presence. The hurt radiating off her was so intense that, if I reached out a hand, I'd be able to feel it.

"People keep telling me that one day this will get easier." She shook her head. "It looks like we're both waiting for that day to come."

I tilted my head from side to side. "I welcome the pain. I deserve it."

Lucy's gaze ran over my face, her forehead wrinkling. "I don't get it?"

"It's easy. I was supposed to look out for Emily. I failed."

A tiny gasp flew from her lips. "Kelvin, you can't blame yourself. What happened to Emily was a horrible, tragic accident, but that's what it was."

"I could have done more to keep her safe. I could have told her not to go out that night."

"Stop! You weren't the one driving the car that hit her. You weren't the guy who'd had too many drinks at his Christmas party and drove drunk. He's paying for that crime. He's the one who should be weighed down with the guilt you carry."

A sharp wedge of tension shifted between my shoulder blades.

Lucy's soft sigh and trembling jaw revealed her own world of hurt. "I thought about visiting him in prison. Ask him why he did it."

I stared at her, my breath hitching. "Did you ever go?"

"No. It wouldn't have done me any good. That guy made a mistake, a huge one, one he's going to live with for the rest of his life. He destroyed his own life because of one horrible, bad decision. He also took away Emily's life."

"And ours," I whispered.

Silence swirled around us like a clogging, toxic mist of misery.

"It seems like that most days," Lucy said on a sigh.

"I don't think I could ever talk to that guy. I'd just hurt him if I got close enough. Make him pay for what he did."

"As tempting as that is, and trust me, I've had plenty of murderous thoughts about him, it would be the last thing Emily would wish for us. Emily hated violence."

I shrugged. I wasn't a fan, either. But every time I thought about that night, arriving on the scene and seeing that drunk guy with his head in his hands as the medics treated his injuries, I felt a flare of rage so hot, it was like a blowtorch searing my heart. Even when he got a twelve-year sentence, it was a hollow victory.

"You're a great guy, Kelvin," Lucy said. "You should focus on something positive about Emily. That's the best way to remember her."

"I do plenty of positive things to remember her. I go to the cemetery every week and talk to her."

"I know you do," she said. "I saw you there on the anniversary of Emily's death."

I crossed my arms over my chest, needing a physical barrier between us. I had to keep my emotions shorn up. The foundations were shaking like a huge earthquake was building. "You did, huh?"

She nodded. "It wasn't the first time. I've seen your parents there, too."

"You never came over to say hi."

"No. That's your time with Emily. It's not for me to intrude."

Lucy had never left my life, even though she hadn't been physically present this past year. All this time, she'd been hiding in the shadows like a tormented ghost. My throat closed up, and I looked away.

"I almost came over when you were there on her anniversary. It looked like you needed a friend. The Christmas wreath you left for Emily was beautiful. She loved the ones made with real holly."

"Yeah, I remember she'd drag me around the Christmas markets to find the perfect wreath. It would drive me crazy the way she inspected twenty different wreaths. They all looked the same to me."

The shiver of a smile crossed Lucy's face. "I leave her a yellow rose when I visit. She loved roses but said the red ones were too cliché. She loved anything that had a sunny color."

"Ah! You're the one leaving the yellow roses," I said. "I keep seeing them. I had no clue who they were from."

"It's my small way of letting Emily know I'm still thinking about her. I'm—" A sob tore from Lucy's lips.

I gathered her into my arms and crushed her against me. She was so tiny, her body shivering as I held her close.

"Sorry." Her voice was muffled against my chest.

"Never apologize for feeling sad that Emily's gone. If you'd replaced her with a new best friend and never talked about her again, that would be something to feel bad about." I ran a hand down her back several times, hoping it would give her comfort.

Slowly, the shaking stopped. Lucy lifted her head. Her dark lashes carried tears as she blinked up at me. Even with sadness etched across her face, she was still pretty, like a china doll. So fragile and easy to break.

I dropped my hold on her and stepped away. I couldn't do this, not with Lucy. My head and heart were all over the place. I longed to open up and share the volcano of feelings inside me, but if I did, everything could burst. If I opened up to Lucy as my heart told me to do, that might be the final thing that busted my emotions wide open. I wasn't ready for that.

Lucy wrapped her arms around her middle as if seeking comfort. "I need to convince Fenella to come home with me. It's best she doesn't stay here overnight. The apartment is getting cold."

"I can put the heating on." I didn't want Lucy to leave. There seemed so much left unsaid. If only I could get the words out without breaking.

"Thanks, but no. Fenella needs to get used to her new home. And I doubt there's anything here she'll eat. She's so fussy."

"I'm sure there's some tinned food in the kitchen. Maybe even tuna."

"She'll turn her nose up at it unless it's sustainably line caught, Atlantic Ocean grown, organic, and served fresh on a china plate." Lucy chuckled. "I've only found one brand of food she'll eat, and I have to hand feed it to her."

"My sister has ruined that cat. What's wrong with some day-old hamburger and a slice of jerky?"

"Fenella would pack up and leave for good if you served her that. I'll go find her." Lucy turned, and I followed her to the door. She'd just pulled it open, when the lights in the apartment blinked out.

I slammed into her back, wrapping my arms around her as I lost my balance, and we pitched to the floor.

Lucy gave an oomph of surprise as we hit the carpet. I rolled, so she was on top of me and I wasn't squashing her. "You okay?"

Her peppermint scented breath drifted across my face. "I think so."

My senses muddled as I breathed in the sweet smell on her breath. "It must be a power cut." I kept a tight hold of Lucy, her slim figure pressed against me.

She was silent for a few seconds. "Maybe we should check it out?"

"Oh! Of course." I'd been holding her way too tight and for too long. I released my grip, missing the feel of her pressed against me as she made her way cautiously to her feet.

I stumbled upright, my insides shaking. What was I doing? I wasn't getting involved with Lucy. Sure, there was an attraction there. I'd always thought she was adorable, but I couldn't let her into my life. I couldn't handle a relationship. There was no way I could risk opening my heart. If I failed someone else I cared about, it would be the end of me.

Chapter 6

Lucy

Hot and cold shivers ran down my body as I forced myself not to fall back into Kelvin's tight embrace. It was so alien to feel such a strong pair of arms wrapped around me.

I hadn't wanted anything to do with anyone for a long time. I'd shut off my emotional tap, even though it occasionally leaked. I didn't want to feel any intense emotions, but everything was bubbling to the surface the more time I spent with him. This was more than just my old crush rearing its head. This felt intense, terrifying, and something I had no control over.

"You weren't hurt when I knocked into you?" Kelvin's voice was low and close to my ear as I fumbled in the dark.

"No. I'm fine. You?" My voice sounded remarkably calm, considering my insides felt like they were on fire.

"I'm good. Stay where you are, so I don't bump into you again."

I blinked as the light from his phone illuminated his face.

"Here, take my hand. I'll lead us back into the living room."

There were a few seconds of fumbling before I clasped his fingers. Warmth trickled up my arm, and my heart beat out an erratic rhythm. It was as if it had gone on a fast spin cycle and rattled inside my chest.

"This isn't good," Kelvin said as we entered the living room. "The street lights are out, too."

He led me to the window, and we stood side-by-side, so close I could feel his warmth.

"You think the power cut has affected the whole town?"

"I don't see any lights out there," he said. "The snow could have brought down some branches on the power lines."

"Maybe I've still got power at mine," I said. "I should go back before it gets any later. And this snow doesn't look like it's stopping anytime soon."

"Driving would be too risky with no street lights," Kelvin said.

"My car headlights will work. I'll take it slow." I needed to get away and put distance between us. I wasn't used to so much intense interaction with one person. But it wasn't just that. It was the desire to stay with Kelvin that scared me the most.

It was my own fault. I'd shut myself away from the world to keep safe. And so far, it had worked. But now, I was exposed to Kelvin's raw intensity, and everything felt messed up.

A screech of tires and the jarring sound of metal grinding together had me jumping. Right outside the apartment, two cars had collided. My stomach pitched to the floor, somersaulted, and shot back up. "Oh my—"

"We need to see if they're okay." Kelvin was already racing to the door, using his phone light to guide him.

My brain wouldn't engage. I couldn't move. My thoughts were yanked back to Emily's car crash. I'd gotten to the scene just before they'd taken her away. I'd seen the carnage, the smashed glass, the torn up metal, the body under the sheet.

"Lucy! People could be hurt." Kelvin had his phone to his ear. "Hello. I need to report an accident."

I shook myself. This wasn't the same thing. I wouldn't let what happened in the past stop me from helping people who could have been injured.

I grabbed my jacket, pulled on my boots, and followed Kelvin down the stairs, the eerie glow from the emergency exit signs the only thing lighting our way.

Fat, white snowflakes swirled around me, and the wind was biting as we headed over to the crash.

Now I was on street level, the accident didn't seem so bad, and my racing heart slowed. One guy looked like he'd slid his car into the other, and the passenger side was dented. People were already out of their cars, apart from one woman who remained in the passenger seat, holding her head.

I hurried over and knelt by her open door. "Are you injured?"

She glanced at me, her eyes huge and her face pale. "I bumped my head on the window. It all happened so fast. We were going slowly, but neither of us could stop in time. The wheels locked. We must have hit ice. I said we shouldn't go out tonight."

"You'll be okay. We've already called for an ambulance. Do you need anything?"

She touched her head and winced. "I'm cold."

"Have you got anything I can use in your trunk?"

"There's a blanket back there."

I grabbed the oversized rough brown blanket from the trunk and covered her with it. "What's your name?"

"Suzie."

"I'm Lucy. I was up in my friend's apartment. We saw what happened."

"It was so scary and loud." Suzie tucked the blanket under her chin. "This is my first car accident."

"Hopefully, it'll be your last," I said. "Hold tight. I can already hear the ambulance."

She gripped my hand as I stood.

"I won't go anywhere. You're safe." The adrenaline racing through my body made me hyper-alert, but I could barely feel the snow as it soaked into my clothing.

Kelvin hurried over. "We've called a tow truck, but they'll be awhile because of the bad weather. If we're careful, we should be able to move the cars so they don't block the road. How are things over here?"

"This is Suzie. She got a bump to the head, but she seems okay. The others?"

"No problems. Mostly shock and a few bruises." He touched my arm. "You good?"

Those two words were loaded with more than a simple check to see how I was doing. He must be remembering Emily's crash as intensely as I was.

A flood of affection poured over me. I was touched that Kelvin was checking in with me. "I've got a handle on it."

He winked. "Same here. This won't take much longer."

Twenty minutes later, the cars had been moved, Suzie was taken away by the ambulance, and everyone else had left.

It was only then that I realized how frozen I was. My hair was soaked, my skin was numb, and I was shaking.

"Come on. We need to get inside before you turn into an icicle," Kelvin said.

I didn't protest as he wrapped an arm around my shoulders and held me close as we hurried back inside the apartment. My numb fingers couldn't handle the zip on my jacket. I stood just inside the front door, dripping water on the floor.

"Let me." Kelvin slid the sodden, freezing jacket off my shoulders. He dropped it to the floor and rubbed my arms with his hands. "Those people got lucky out there."

I nodded, wanting nothing more than to sink against his warmth.

"Jeez! Your lips are blue. You'll end up in the hospital if you don't get warm." Kelvin stepped away. "I'll find you a towel for your hair. Then you're drinking as much tea as I can get down you. And take off as many wet clothes as you can."

"I'm not getting naked. I'll freeze."

He slowed and turned back to me. "And all of Emily's clothes are gone." He pulled off his jacket and yanked off his sweater, leaving him in a black T-shirt. He held it out to me.

"You'll be too cold without it." My fingers inched toward the sweater.

"I've got more meat on me than you. Go get changed in the bathroom."

I stumbled into the bathroom, pulled off my damp sweater and T-shirt, and pulled his sweater over my head. It swamped me, but it was warm, dry, and smelt of his musky cologne. I closed my eyes and breathed it in, imagining him holding me again.

I shook my head. "Idiot."

"Is everything good in there?" Kelvin knocked on the door.

I jumped. "Fine. I'll be right out." I pulled off my wet sweatpants. Kelvin's sweater was almost to my knees, so it would cover my modesty. I pulled up my thick, knee-length purple socks and left the bathroom.

He passed me a mug of something steaming. "Tea. No milk, but this will warm you up."

My teeth chattered. "How did you make it without any power?"

"The gas hob is still working. And I've got matches." His gaze ran over my outfit. "Love the socks."

I sipped the welcoming warm liquid. "I always come prepared. My feet get easily cold."

"They suit you."

I wasn't certain if that was a compliment or if he was teasing me.

We walked into the living room, and I looked around. There was only one chair.

Kelvin nodded at the chair before sitting beside it, his own drink in hand.

My gaze went to the window where the snow still fell. "Maybe you're right about not leaving here tonight."

"Neither of us should go anywhere until the snow stops, the power's back on, and a snowplow has been by. We've just seen how dangerous it is out there."

I lifted a hand. "I'm not fighting you on that. Seeing that crash and the mangled cars, it, well, you can guess what it reminded me of."

He nodded. "At least they all got to walk away."

We sat beside each other, Kelvin on the floor and me in the chair, slowly warming up.

"Do you need anything else?" he asked.

"Actually, I'm starving," I said. "I can't remember the last time I ate."

"Food?" He tapped his chin with a finger. "You're presenting me with a challenge. Mom's not gotten around to clearing everything from the kitchen cupboards. Let's see what we've got." He stood and headed back to the kitchen.

I took a few more sips of my drink, the warmth taking the aching cold out of my fingers, before following him.

"Did you find anything?" My stomach growled.

He grinned at me before continuing his hunt through the kitchen cupboards. "We have tuna. There's some dried pasta, which I could cook in the water on the stove. Not much to go with it, though. There are also tins of beans."

"It all sounds good. I'd eat the pasta dry if I have to."

"It won't come to that. There are some herbs and a tin of tomatoes. Let's see what I can make with that."

I set down my mug and turned away, an excited flutter in my stomach. "I wonder..."

Kelvin grabbed my mug and refilled it. "What do you wonder?"

"Our candy cache." I walked toward Emily's bedroom. "Did you find it?"

"You've lost me."

I grinned and hugged myself as I hurried to the bedroom. "Come with me. I bet it's still there."

Footsteps followed me into the bedroom as I knelt and pressed against a small wall panel. It was stiff, but it pushed out. I laughed as I saw the contents. "Emily's looking out for us." I reached in and pulled out several bars of chocolate.

Kelvin was silent for a second before a deep, rumbling laugh came out of him. It sent tingles down my spine to my toes and back to the top of my head, warming me more than the tea.

"You two had a secret candy stash?"

I stood and handed him a bar of chocolate. "We had one at school. It was at the back of the library. We used to stash candy there and sneak it out when we were supposed to be studying. No one ever found it. It was at the bottom of a book stack. You had to push the panel and force your hand in. When Emily got this place, she said she wanted to keep the tradition going. This was the perfect location. I know it was silly, but—"

"No, it's great. And you're right. Emily's watching over us, making sure we don't have to force down a bland pasta dinner with no dessert afterward."

"It's more like a late-night snack." I broke off a chunk of chocolate and bit into it. It was Emily's favorite, salted caramel.

"You're right," Kelvin said. "It looks like we're spending the night here."

I swallowed, a shiver of anxiety running through me. Kelvin was a friend, and I could handle spending a night in the same apartment as him. It didn't mean anything.

The trouble was, it did. I'd locked my emotions away so tightly that they threatened to overspill. Kelvin was kind, thoughtful, and even more handsome than the last time I'd seen him. But I couldn't do this. I had to protect my heart. It wasn't open to getting hurt again.

"Why don't we take our late-night snack into the living room?" Kelvin said.

I nodded, grabbed the rest of the candy, and replaced the panel. I rested my hand against it. "Thanks, Emily." My smile was bittersweet as I returned to the living room and sat next to Kelvin. Him on the floor again and me taking the chair.

We were quiet as we ate the chocolate and waited for the pasta to cook. There'd been a shift between Kelvin and me. I'd felt so alone after losing Emily and had assumed that no one felt the same way I did. Kelvin was proving me wrong. Of course, he was heartbroken over what had happened. He missed Emily as much as I did. It was something we shared, but it was more than that. We'd been friends when growing up. He'd always been around, and my teenage crush had been strong. The adult crush felt stronger, real, and way more intense.

"Hey, look. Fenella's made an appearance." Kelvin pointed to the door where the little cat stood, watching us.

She was just the distraction I needed. I placed my chocolate down and jumped up. "Let's see if I can get her to eat. She must be hungry, too." I dashed into the kitchen, found a can of tuna, grateful it had a pull tab, and opened it. I discovered an old plate, placed some tuna on it, and set it on the floor.

"Fenella, do you want something to eat?" I made kissing noises until she appeared in the doorway.

She wandered over, ate a couple of mouthfuls of tuna, and turned away, heading back into the bedroom.

I walked into the living room and stood in the doorway. "I never asked you. You don't want Fenella, do you?"

Kelvin's eyebrows shot up, and he shook his head. "She's a cute cat, but why would I want her?"

"I wondered if you considered her a link to Emily." I didn't want to give up Fenella, but I wouldn't keep her if she'd give comfort to Emily's family. After all, I was used to being on my own.

"No. I mean, I remember Emily being crazy about that cat. She was cat mad ever since we were kids. Fenella's yours if you want her."

"I do, but I'm not sure she's sold on me just yet." I looked at the bedroom, but the cat had vanished from view.

"Did you know Emily left money in her will to Forever Paws?" Kelvin said.

I huffed out a breath. "I'm not surprised, especially since that's where I found Fenella. It seems like Christmas magic stepped in and joined us."

"Christmas magic?"

I walked over and picked up my chocolate. "That's what the lady at the animal shelter said. Something about Christmas magic and sprinkling it over everything. It didn't make much sense at the time, but it makes you wonder. Fenella had been at Forever Paws all this time, and no one else chose to take her home. She's a pretty cat. You'd think someone would try to bring her out of her shell. Then Emily left them money after she died. Maybe there is some kind of weird connection."

"Or maybe it's all a coincidence, and there's no such thing as Christmas magic," Kelvin said, his tone gruff.

Was this a coincidence? Emily had been a huge fan of Christmas. She'd believed anything was possible at Christmas time.

I settled back in the seat, closed my eyes, and sucked on a piece of chocolate. Kelvin was right. There was nothing magical about this time of year. No amount of glitter, tinsel, or twinkling trees could change things.

And as much as I wanted to, I couldn't get involved with Kelvin or his family. My heart wouldn't take it. It was only just beating in its current state. Opening it up and risking getting hurt again was too dangerous.

I'd stick with the real Christmas. No matter how cold, bleak, and lonely that felt.

Chapter 7

♥

Fenella

When I finally found my way back to Emily's apartment, I was so excited that the very tip of my tail had wiggled. I was finally home. I'd get to see Emily after all this time, snuggle against her softness, and let her stroke me until I was drooling with happiness.

I hunted and hunted for her. The place still smelt like her, but it wasn't a fresh scent. Emily smelt of sugar, creamy coffee, and flowers. It was a pretty intense smell for a cat's nose, but I adored it. Whenever I got that heady whiff, I knew she was nearby and would hop up for a cuddle.

But the smells I associated with Emily seemed stale. And she was nowhere to be found.

That wasn't the only unsettling thing about my home. Everything had been moved. My favorite couch with the squashy cushions was missing, my food bowl wasn't in its usual position, full of delicious treats, and there was no sign of a litter tray. Where had my things gone? And where were Emily's things?

I called for her until my throat hurt, but she didn't show up. I'd keep calling until I lost my meow if it meant she'd hear me.

I stamped on the old sweater I'd discovered at the back of the closet. A piece of the wool had come loose, and I'd been chewing on it. There was something delicious about chewing on wool; the way it rubbed against my teeth felt divine.

But even this wasn't a comfort. Neither was the poor quality tinned tuna Lucy had tried to make me eat. I was hungry enough to eat a small amount but only to stop my stomach from complaining.

Twice, I'd crept from my hiding place and listened to Lucy and Kelvin talk about missing Emily. They said some strange things that I didn't understand. Why had she left money to Forever Paws? Was it because she was grateful they'd looked after me all this time?

I'd have preferred her to take care of me, but maybe she hadn't been able to.

When I saw her again, I'd make sure she knew she didn't need to give money to Forever Paws. I had a long list of things I wanted and was happy for Emily to buy them for me. I hadn't forgotten my old friend, Tabby, and her amazing drinking fountain. Free flowing water always available whenever she wanted it. That looked like something I'd enjoy. Plus, Emily always ran out of catnip. I got through mountains of the stuff, couldn't get enough of it, and I was sure you could bulk buy it. Emily could pay to have a daily delivery of catnip sent here.

My back felt stiff. I'd been snuggled on this old sweater for ages, not inclined to move. I slid out of the closet and had a long stretch, arching my back until my jaw hit the floor, before silently padding back to the living room.

The door was open, and I spied an enormous moon high in the sky. I'd sometimes watch the moon with Emily. She'd tell me the tale of how men flew up there like giant birds and landed on it. I had no idea how they did that. Humans didn't have wings or feathers. But I believed Emily. She was right about everything, even though she occasionally bought me the wrong brand of cat food. I forgave her for those little mishaps.

I settled on the carpet, my gaze shifting to Lucy. She'd always been nice to me, and I'd visited her apartment before Emily vanished.

Emily had a wonderful wheeled device she'd put me in to take me long distances. She said it was nice to get fresh air rather than going in the car. I wasn't certain about it at first, but it was enclosed, warm, and soft. And I got to take in all my surroundings with zero chance of encountering a dog or an unfriendly cat. I wasn't much of a fighter and avoided conflict when possible. It always messed up my beautiful fur, and I'd have to spend hours grooming to get every piece back in place.

I remembered Lucy as happier than she was now. And she didn't have those lines across her forehead that never seemed to go away.

Since I'd been at her apartment, she'd barely noticed me. Not like Emily. Emily noticed everything I did. She praised me when I used my litter tray, she'd tell me what a good girl I was when

I finished the food in my bowl, and she'd spend at least half an hour every evening grooming my silky fur until it shone. She was the perfect human.

The way Lucy and Kelvin kept talking about Emily, I knew she was close by. Maybe she'd been ill and had gone away to get better. I'd had a cold once, so I knew how awful you felt when you got sick. You don't want to do anything other than sleep and get cuddles. But Emily would be back. I just knew it. I had to be patient.

Finally, I was home, and I was happy about that, even though it felt weird and everything was out of place.

I returned to the closet and snuggled back on the old sweater, grabbing a piece of wool and sucking on it. It was such a comforting thing to do, it made my body feel like liquid, and my eyes closed.

Humans said that magic happened at Christmas. I wasn't sure what magic was, but it often involved gifts, lots of sparkly things, and people laughing and hugging each other. Maybe that Christmas magic would include Emily coming back to me. She was the best hugger.

Hugs with Emily, fresh chicken, and a big bag of catnip. That would make all my Christmas wishes come true.

Chapter 8

Kelvin

My eyes flicked open. For a few seconds, I had no idea where I was, other than that it was freezing. I rolled over, my back not happy I'd spent the night on the floor. Then it rushed back to me. I'd stayed overnight at Emily's apartment.

My calf bumped against something warm. I glanced down to see Fenella sleeping next to me.

She lifted her head and blinked before settling back down, her tail flipping over her nose.

"I guess you got cold last night, too." I rolled into a sitting position, my gaze going to the window. It looked like we were trapped inside a snow globe.

I stood and eased the kinks out of my back before walking to the window. Snow was piled up everywhere. A good five feet of fresh snow had fallen overnight. The road looked impassable, and several cars had been abandoned, parked poorly so their rear ends stuck out.

I'd used the cushions from the chair as a makeshift bed in the living room but hadn't gotten much sleep. I'd kept thinking about Lucy in the bedroom on her own. It had taken me a while to convince her to take the only mattress in the place. No way was she sleeping on the floor.

I'd wanted to stay with her. She was getting to me. I knew the signs. I'd felt attraction before, but this was different. It felt new and intense. I couldn't develop feelings for Lucy. She wasn't in the right place for a relationship. Neither was I.

I swiftly used the bathroom then headed to the bedroom, cracking the door open an inch.

Lucy was curled in a tight ball, a blanket wrapped around her. One hand poked out from under the blanket.

Since talking to her about Emily, the pain in my chest had faded. It was still there, but it was muted. Lucy was good for me, and I wanted to keep her in my life. But... what if I failed her just as I had Emily? I knew the consequences of not being around to protect the people I loved. I couldn't lose anyone else.

I walked over and touched her hand. It was icy cold. I shouldn't have left her alone last night. I wouldn't have minded if she'd used my body warmth. The idea of curling up around Lucy was way too appealing for its own good.

I clasped her hand between mine to warm it.

Lucy's head jerked up. Two dark, confused eyes blinked open and stared at me.

"Hey. I didn't mean to startle you. You're freezing." I rubbed her hand between mine.

Recognition dawned in her eyes, and she pulled the blanket down an inch. "What time is it?"

"Just gone seven."

Her gaze flicked to our entwined hands. "I got so cold in the night. I couldn't get warm."

I continued rubbing her hand. Her bed messy hair and tired eyes did nothing to take away the attraction I felt.

"I'm warmer now." Lucy grinned as she gave me her other hand. "This one could do with warming up, though."

I took her icy hand in mine. "Happy to be of service."

"Still no power?"

"Nope. Everything is still out. I just looked out the window, and no one has their Christmas lights sparkling."

"How did you sleep?" she asked.

"Not great. I woke to find Fenella next to me. She finally came out of her hiding place."

"That poor cat must be so confused. I'm not sure she understands that Emily is never coming back."

"She kept meowing when I first let her in the apartment. I think she was calling for Emily." I kept Lucy's hand between mine, even though it was warm. She didn't object.

"Hopefully, she'll get used to being with me."

"You'll take great care of her. Just like Emily did."

Lucy nodded. "She adored that cat. She called her a fur baby. Said cats were almost as amazing as new born babies."

"Hah! I've heard that once or twice. She'd always threaten to adopt a dozen cats and not provide grandchildren when Mom got too nosy about her love life."

Lucy's chuckle sent a flush of comforting warmth through me.

"You know, Emily once suggested that I date you," I said.

Lucy's eyes widened. "She never told me."

"Probably because there was a big caveat. She said I could only date you if I promised to marry you."

Laughter burst out of Lucy. She sat up and faced me. "I can just imagine her doing that. She was always looking out for me. She used to vet every guy I dated."

That idea didn't sit well with me. Of course, Lucy would have dated in the past, but I didn't want her to be with anyone else. For all I knew, she could have someone in her life, and there was no hope for us. Us. There was no us.

"How old were you when Emily suggested that?" Lucy asked.

"I was fourteen, and you were twelve. At the time, I figured I was too young to make such a commitment. Emily said that was the deal. Marriage or nothing."

Lucy laughed again.

"Are you seeing anyone?" I asked as casually as I could. "I know you're not married. Emily would have talked non-stop about the wedding."

"And I'd have picked her as my bridesmaid, so you'd probably have been dragged to a couple of dress fittings too. I bet you're sorry you missed that."

"I wouldn't have minded. Emily would have looked ridiculous in a pink fluffy dress."

"Hey! My bridesmaids will look stunning when the time comes. And I wouldn't have dressed Emily in anything pink or fluffy."

We grinned as we shared this happy fantasy.

"So, no marriage on the cards?" I asked.

"It never happened for me." She shrugged. "I've been single three years."

That comment almost floored me. "Why?"

She looked away. "I never met the right guy. I date, but guys my age are still into partying and drinking too much."

"You like to party. You used to go out with Emily to those over-priced cocktail bars."

"Sure, but not when the parties involve beer kegs and hooking up with someone random."

"Those kinds of parties exist for people over the age of twenty-one?"

Her smile was wry. "Unfortunately, they do. I went to a couple with previous dates. They made me feel young again and not in a good way."

I nodded slowly. "You always were intense, even when we were kids."

"That's a bad thing? I see no problem in not getting wasted and high every weekend."

I lifted a hand. "I never said it was a problem. My mom used to say you had an old soul."

"I like to think I matured young."

"That works, too." Her glare had me chuckling.

"I like fun, but the quiet kind these days," Lucy said. "I like being home. I need someone who likes to hang out, watch a movie, or cook a meal together. That kind of thing. Most guys find that dull. Anyone who thinks jetting off to Vegas at the last minute is fun, isn't the right guy for me."

"Not everyone is into that sort of thing. I want a relationship like my parents. They're great together, even after all these years. They made an amazing home for Emily and me. It was a safe place, and they always made sure we knew we were loved, even when we messed up."

"I always enjoyed hanging out at your house," Lucy said. "My parents were so busy, we only really talked at the weekends. Your parents are amazing. Your dad even gave me career advice. He helped me figure out my path as a designer."

"I never knew that."

"He saw that I was really into drawing and asked what I planned to do with my talent. I told him I had no idea. I didn't think you could make a career out of drawing. You always hear about starving artists having to work bar jobs to pay the bills. Your dad suggested getting into book cover design. I hadn't even thought about it before, but of course, someone has to design those covers. I looked into it, and that's what led me to do my degree. Thanks to your dad, I got to run my own business, made it a success, and do the creative work I love."

My heart warmed as Lucy spoke so highly of my dad. He was an awesome guy, and our family setup was amazing. At least, it had been until it got blown apart a year ago. Since then, we'd been stumbling around, trying to find how the pieces fit when a vital one was missing.

"You haven't met anyone through work?" I asked.

"That's the tricky thing, working for myself and from home. It means I don't get to see many people. Most of my interactions are online or on the phone. I occasionally go to design conferences, but the conversations tend to be work focused."

I pulled my hands away from Lucy's. For a second, I'd wondered if I was the right guy for her. I shook my head, a flame of rage curling inside me. It had been dormant for hours, but I couldn't get used to that feeling.

I was an idiot for letting down my guard. What if I asked her out and something bad happened once I'd fallen for her? Another accident I couldn't control. Or Lucy could get sick. I wouldn't be able to keep her safe.

I shook myself, hating the indecision fighting inside me. I knew my path. It wasn't with Lucy, no matter how tempted I was.

"Emily always said I needed to wait for the perfect guy. Someone who'd watch out for me. She said I'd know him when I saw him," Lucy said.

Something hard and painful lodged in my throat. "Emily was always overly romantic when it came to love. Even though her choice in guys was terrible."

"She could have dated the most wonderful guy in the world, and you wouldn't have liked him," she said.

"You're probably right. But she gave you solid advice. Don't settle for anyone who doesn't make you happy." I reached out to take her hand again but pulled back. I couldn't make Lucy happy, not when there was a hole where my heart should be.

"What about you?" Her voice was soft. "Emily never said much about who you're dating."

"I'm not. There's not been anyone for a while." And there never would be.

"You don't get... lonely?"

"Do you?"

Her gaze met mine, loaded with emotions I was too worked up to decipher. "Sometimes. But it's easier being alone."

I hated the image of Lucy sitting alone in her messy apartment with no one checking up on her. It was wrong. She should be surrounded by love. She should have guys clamoring at her door, wanting to be in her life and make her happy. But I couldn't be that guy.

I needed to get out of here. I stood and stepped away. "I was thinking of walking to the nearest gas station. There's one half a mile from here."

"How's that going to help us?" She struggled to her feet, the blanket wrapped around her shoulders.

"They may know something about when the snowplows are getting here and we can leave."

"You don't want to go out there. You'll freeze." She followed me as I headed to the door, my steps rapid. I had to get away. All my tangled feelings wanted to burst out, and I couldn't let them.

"I need some air, anyway. And it's stopped snowing. It'll be okay." I said.

She was quiet as I pulled on my boots. "What's wrong?"

"Nothing's wrong. I just need..." What did I need? Lucy's gentle ways had gotten under my skin. If things had been different, if I hadn't known her most of my life, this wouldn't matter. But she'd slotted back in as if no time had passed between us. And although some of our shared memories were bittersweet, I didn't want to let Lucy go.

"Just like you told me we could talk if ever I needed to, the same goes for you," Lucy said. "I feel different since you came to my apartment with Emily's things. I can't explain it, but lighter somehow. Does that make sense?"

"I'm glad I helped you." I focused on lacing my boots, ignoring the shaking inside me.

I was almost out the door, when her hand settled on my shoulder. It tipped me over the edge. Something cracked inside me. I heard it shatter.

I'd been stuck for so long, trapped in my misery, unable to move forward. Now everything I held onto so tightly was about to explode, and Lucy would take its full force.

Chapter 9

Lucy

It cut into me like a jagged, rusty knife to see Kelvin hurting so badly. I took his hand, being careful to keep mine steady, unlike my heart, which careened in my chest and made me dizzy.

"Emily's death wasn't your fault," I said.

"I should have been there for her." His body slumped forward, curling in on itself. "I was supposed to protect her."

"You weren't to know what would happen that night." I tugged his hand, and after a few seconds of resistance, he followed me into the living room.

I placed the cushions back on the chair and forced him to sit before settling on the arm next to him and taking his hand back in mine. I had to anchor him to me before he drifted away. I'd sensed that, if he'd walked out the door, that would have ended whatever was building between us. Maybe I should have let him go, but I couldn't.

"It was my job to keep Emily safe," he said. "I was her big brother."

"And I was her best friend. Maybe I should have told her not to go out that night. I should have known something bad would happen."

"You couldn't have known that."

"Exactly. Just as you couldn't have known that guy would drink too much and get behind the wheel of his car."

"I could have driven her," Kelvin said. "She texted me that day to let me know she planned some last minute shopping. She'd seen a bargain she wanted to grab and couldn't wait."

"I could have done exactly the same. And I could have told her to go the next morning or ordered online and paid extra for shipping, so it got to her in time for Christmas."

"I should have told Emily to save her money and not spend it on the family. I should have told her that having her there on Christmas Day was more important than some cut-price gift."

I sucked in a breath. "And I could have not shown her those bargains online. If I hadn't done that, she'd have never left her apartment."

"I bet Emily would have found them, anyway," Kelvin said. "She loved bargain hunting."

"Maybe, maybe not."

"This isn't your fault," Kelvin said after a long pause.

"That's my point," I said. "Neither of us knew what would happen. It doesn't mean I don't feel regret every day and play the 'what if' game until I feel sick, but we didn't have control over that situation. We don't always know what's around the corner."

His gaze locked onto mine, and the anger and pain shining from his eyes made my heart stumble.

"Is that why you're not around anymore?" he said.

"What do you mean?"

"You stopped being a part of the family?"

Sadness ran over me like acid rain, making me itch and tingle. "I didn't mean to shut you all out. You needed time to grieve. I didn't want to get in the way."

"So did you. We could have done that together."

A band of pain tightened around my chest, and I squeezed Kelvin's hand. "I loved Emily so much. When I lost her, I couldn't imagine letting anyone else into my life. I wouldn't have been able to handle it if they'd left me or something bad happened to them."

Kelvin lowered his head and rested his other hand over mine. "I never want to risk failing anyone again. That's why I haven't been dating. I didn't want to get close to someone and then let them down or have something bad happen to them. I'd tear myself apart trying to figure out how I could have prevented it."

His tender admission made my heart quiver. "You've not gotten involved with anyone because you didn't want to let them down?"

He nodded. "It seems like that's what we've both been doing. Existing in this world but not really living."

"I guess so." Those words stung, but there was a horrible truth inside them. I'd been going through the motions for a long time, doing my work, keeping myself just about together, but nothing else. I hadn't experienced a moment of pleasure this past year. Every time I looked at the world, it appeared bleak and barren. When I saw people enjoying themselves, wrapped in their own bubble of happiness and not grieving the way I was, it was too painful. I'd had to step away.

"Thanks, Lucy." Kelvin's voice was so soft I could barely hear him.

"What for?"

"Being as messed up as me when it comes to Emily." He lifted his head, and my heart seized as I saw the tears on his cheeks.

I reached over and brushed them away. "From one messed up person to another, you're welcome."

He choked out a laugh and scrubbed a hand across his face. "I haven't been able to talk about this, not like I can with you. I can't talk to Mom and Dad; they're so fragile. If they realized I was struggling, it would destroy them. I've talked to friends, and they say the right words, but they don't get it. You do. You were there. You loved Emily as much as I did."

"I did. I still love her." A void inside me faded as I stared into his shining blue eyes. "I know one thing Emily would have hated. To see us wrapped in our own misery, not living our lives."

"I don't want to forget her," he said. "If I start living again, she'll move away from me."

I knelt in front of him and took his face in my hands. "You'll never forget her. Maybe you'll forget the pain, which is a good thing, but she'll always be with you. Just like she's always with me." I reached for the locket I never took off and opened it. In one side, there was a picture of a smiling Emily.

Kelvin lifted the locket and stared at it. "For so long, I felt like I deserved this pain because I let Emily down."

"I know that feeling only too well." We were so close, I could feel his pulse racing in his wrist. "I also know this isn't what Emily would want for either of us. Of course, she'd want us to miss her, but it would break her heart to see us like this. And she'd do everything in her power to change it. Even wear a fluffy pink dress and dance around for you."

He huffed out a soft laugh. "Maybe that's what we need to do then. Stop being sad. But I'll never stop missing her."

"Neither will I."

He closed the locket. "You only have one picture in there."

"This locket is for the people I love the most." I rested my hand over it.

Kelvin touched my face, stroking his fingers down my cheek and leaving behind a trail of heat.

I leaned into his touch, terrified of crossing this line, but not able to stop myself.

"Lucy, I wish I'd done more to make sure you were okay after Emily's death. I was so caught up in my own grief that—"

I pressed a finger against his lips. "I never expected anything from you. Our worlds were shattered. I don't think I got out of bed for a week. Emily's funeral forced me into the outside world, and after I'd experienced how painful it was being on my own without her, I decided I didn't want anything to do with it. I hid away. I chose to do that to keep myself safe."

"Do you feel safe?" His gaze went to my lips.

The question pounded at me, my vision blurring and my brain refusing to cooperate. "I did for a while."

"And now?" He leaned toward me, so close. His breath streaked across my sensitive skin.

"Now, nothing feels safe. And I'll admit I'm terrified about what to do next."

As Kelvin leaned closer, I closed my eyes. I needed this. I'd been so long without anyone in my life. And Kelvin understood me. He understood everything I'd gone through and wasn't judging me. He'd understand when I still had dark days and had to retreat from everything. But I got the feeling he'd also be there if I stayed in that dark place for too long, encouraging me out, encouraging me to see what the world had to offer. What it had to offer with him in it.

A loud whirring sound and a light flicking on had me blinking and jerking away. I looked up to see the bare bulb on the ceiling was on.

"Hey! The power's back." Kelvin looked around the room before his gaze met mine.

I nodded and stood, my body uncomfortably warm and my knees shaking.

"I'll see if the boiler's working and get some heat in this place." He touched my arm before leaving the room.

I sucked in a breath, unfamiliar with the sense of lightness inside me. Things had changed between Kelvin and me. I wasn't sure where this was heading or even where it would end up, but for the first time in a long time, I was excited about exploring the possibilities.

I didn't want to leave, not when things had just gotten started.

I made coffee for both of us and left Kelvin a mug on the counter as I went to search for Fenella.

She was tucked at the back of the closet, snuggled on an old sweater that must have been missed when Kelvin and his parents were packing up Emily's clothes.

I knelt and gently stroked her head. "You're not going to like me for this, but we'll have to leave soon. This isn't your home anymore. Your home's with me. I hope you can be happy in my apartment. It won't be the same as it was with Emily, but I'll take the best care of you."

Fenella lifted her head and regarded me with calm eyes.

"I'll even push you around in your cat pram. And I won't mind if the neighbors laugh and call me a crazy cat lady."

Fenella uncurled, stretched, and stepped out of the closet. She looked around the bedroom and then at me, before softly rubbing the side of her face against my hand.

That small show of affection had tears falling down my cheeks. I had no idea if Fenella experienced grief or loss, but maybe she'd accepted me and accepted that, if she was to find happiness, she had to do things differently. Just like I did. She had to let people into her life and trust them not to leave.

My frozen, broken heart felt in rhythm for the first time in a year. It was because of Kelvin but also Fenella. I was finally letting people, and animals, into my life again after so long isolating myself.

Should I risk more? Should I let Kelvin know how I felt about him?

"What do you say, Fenella?" I scratched behind her ears. "Or are you enough of a Christmas gift for me?"

Fenella head-butted my hand again before staring at me and flicking her tail. She looked like she understood what I was saying.

"Lucy, there's a snowplow coming along the road. We should be able to get out of here soon," Kelvin called from the kitchen.

The moment for sharing my sparking, scary emotions had passed.

"Great. I'll get my things together and settle Fenella." I pulled on my boots and jacket and turned to the cat who'd followed me into the hallway. "How about we try something new?"

I collected the cat carrier I'd brought with me and opened it.

Fenella stared at the carrier for several long seconds.

"I got pink, just like Emily would have chosen for you." As if a cat cared what color her carrier was.

Fenella sniffed around it and then looked up, as if waiting for me to do something.

"I know. It's different for both of us." I stroked along her silky back. "It's just you and me and our memories of Emily. Will that do?"

After giving the cat carrier another sniff, Fenella stepped inside, turned in a circle, and lay down.

I couldn't believe my luck. Or maybe it was Emily, looking on and giving Fenella a gentle nudge in the right direction.

I carried Fenella into the living room and took one last look around the apartment. Sadness and acceptance filtered through me. It was time to move on.

Chapter 10

♥

Kelvin

"Are you certain you want to do this?" I sat back on my couch, my phone by my ear.

"We should do something." Mom's voice was quiet but determined. "Even if it's just the three of us sitting down to have lunch together. We can't let the day go unnoticed."

I thought about suggesting Lucy come for Christmas lunch. She'd been on my mind these past two days since we'd been snowed in at Emily's apartment.

"Please come. It'll mean a lot to your father."

"You sure about that? I doubt he'll even notice it's Christmas Day."

"He will. We both want you here."

As much as I wanted to pretend Christmas wasn't around the corner, I wouldn't let my parents down. "Lunch will be good. But let's not make a big deal out of this. Keep it simple."

"I understand. None of us feel much like celebrating, but Emily did love Christmas. I can imagine how unhappy she'd be about us not doing anything."

My bare, decoration-free apartment taunted me as I looked around it. I hadn't bothered putting up a single decoration. Emily always bullied me into getting tons of tinsel, flashing lights, and a snow frosted tree. This year, everything Christmas themed remained in storage.

"I haven't gotten gifts for anyone," I said.

"You being here is all the gift we need," Mom said. "Get here for noon. We'll have a nice lunch together and maybe go for a walk in the afternoon if the snow holds off. You can stay over if you like."

"Sure. That sounds great. I'll see you tomorrow."

Mom sucked in a breath. This conversation wasn't over. "Are you doing anything this evening?"

Again, I thought about Lucy. She'd be on her own tonight, just like me. "Nothing special." When Lucy wasn't around, it felt like I was missing something. It wasn't just because of her link to Emily. I'd been drawn to her quiet intensity before, and those long dark lashes always made me look twice.

"Don't sit in on your own," Mom said. "It's not good for you."

"What are you and Dad doing tonight?"

A soft sigh slid along the line. "We're different. We're old and set in our ways. Parties aren't for us. They take too long to recover from."

I huffed out a quiet laugh. "Mom, you've got plenty of life left in you. Certainly enough to go out for a Christmas Eve drink with Dad."

"I'll be busy, especially now we're having lunch tomorrow. I have things to prepare."

"I did say a simple lunch. Don't get stressed over this."

"No, I won't. I want to make it nice, though." She sighed again. "I'll worry about you if you don't do anything on Christmas Eve."

"It's too late to go anywhere," I said. "I don't want to go to a bar. Maybe I'll go see a movie."

"On your own? You could come here this evening. I know it's not what the cool kids would do, hang out with their parents on Christmas Eve, but—"

"Mom! Really, I'm doing okay." I scrubbed a hand down my face, searching for a change of topic. "Hey, I forgot to tell you, Lucy found Emily's cat at an animal shelter. She's adopted her."

She gasped. "Fenella? That's extraordinary. I often wondered what happened to that little cutie. When she disappeared, I figured she must have gotten lost or maybe injured. You say Lucy has taken her on?"

"That's right. She's had her a couple of weeks."

"It's a Christmas miracle they found each other. Emily adored that cat." Mom was quiet for a second. "How's Lucy doing? I've not seen her since the funeral. I called her a few times, but I got the impression she didn't want to stay in touch."

"I'm sure she does want to see you. She's just... you know, finding things tough."

"I miss her," Mom said. "She was so close with Emily. I'm glad she found Fenella. Is Lucy seeing anyone?"

There was no way I was diving into that thorny topic. Mom was always on the hunt for a girlfriend for me and proposing her friends' single daughters as potential dates. "Mom, I've got to go. I've got plans to make for this evening, since I don't get to hang out by myself."

"I'm just asking because I want to make sure Lucy's happy. I expect she's seeing her family tomorrow."

I huffed out a breath. She wasn't. She'd be on her own all day.

"If Lucy wants to come to lunch with us, she'd be welcome. I know you two—"

"Gotta go, Mom. Love you." I ended the call and set my phone down. I shouldn't have mentioned Lucy. Mom used to love dropping not so innocent comments about what a sweet girl she was, and didn't I think she was pretty?

I thought both those things and a lot more about Lucy.

I glanced around my bare apartment again. I shouldn't sit here on my own on Christmas Eve. There'd been no new snow over the last two days, so I had no excuse to stay in because of the weather, but I'd turned down the invitations to go out with friends. I didn't want to face all that joy.

I pulled up my messages and opened one to Lucy. *How's Fenella doing?*

The response was almost instant. *Take a look for yourself.* She'd attached a picture of Fenella looking grumpy and wearing a small Santa hat.

I chuckled as I typed. *She looks full of the joy of Christmas.*

She's getting there. She's eating more and has explored the whole apartment. She still spends a lot of time in the closet but seems more content.

That's good to hear. What plans have you got tonight? Going out?

Finishing a book cover to send to a client as an early Christmas present.

My pulse skipped a beat. *After that?*

I'm giving a talk at Trenton College at seven. They've had a few problems with students drunk driving. They asked me to tell them my story.

On Christmas Eve? I gripped the edge of the couch. I wasn't brave enough to talk about what happened to Emily to a bunch of strangers.

It's important. We don't want anyone to wake up on Christmas morning, their lives changed forever like ours were a year ago.

The air in my apartment seemed thin. I took several long, deep breaths to slow my hammering heart. Lucy was doing an amazing thing, sharing her pain and loss to make sure tragedy didn't strike others.

I bet they'll all be on apple juice after you've talked to them.

Here's hoping. Or at least, be sensible.

My fingers hovered over the phone. There was so much more I wanted to say. I wanted Lucy to know that I hadn't stopped thinking about her. I needed her to be happy again. She'd been frozen in time ever since Emily died. And I was the same.

Her pain had shone a spotlight on my struggle. After spending time with her, it had been like a sledgehammer to the gut. I hadn't been happy for a year. But now... there was something about Lucy. Something that made me want to take a risk. See if my heart could stand it.

Have a good Christmas, Lucy. I sent the message. The real conversation I wanted to have with her shouldn't be done over text. Maybe it shouldn't be done at all.

Thanks. Will you have a good Christmas?

"I'll try," I muttered. Rather than telling her about my struggle, I kept things light.

Sure. Spending it with Mom and Dad. Should I ask her to come with me?

Good plan. Have a nice day tomorrow. She signed off with a single kiss, a signal that the conversation was over.

I set my phone down, stood, and walked to the window. It was dark outside, and a light frost sprinkled the top of the snow. The night sky was clear, and a star streaked across the vast expanse of deep blue.

In the distance, there was a faint jingle of sleigh bells. I looked around to see who was outside but couldn't spot anyone.

"Christmas magic," I whispered. "Do I believe in it?"

Before I had a chance to talk myself out of what I was about to do, I grabbed my keys, pulled on my jacket and boots, and headed to my car. The college Lucy was talking at was less than a half-hour drive away.

She wasn't giving her presentation for another two hours. That gave me just enough time to find some gifts for my parents, grab a bite to eat, and drop by and see her talk.

I couldn't let this opportunity pass. I'd been on my own for long enough. I hadn't paid attention to any woman until I saw Lucy. Things had to change. I felt ready to move on. It didn't mean I'd forget Emily, not for a second. She'd always be in my heart and in my thoughts, but Lucy could be there, too.

With a smile on my face and my steps lighter than they'd been for a long time, I headed out to see if there was some magic to be had at Christmas.

I was late getting to the lecture room where Lucy was giving her talk. The stores had been insanely busy, with stressed out gift hunters chasing down the last present with ruthless precision and a fair amount of cussing. People who left their Christmas shopping to the last minute must have something wrong with them. I was never doing that again.

But the stress had been worth it. I'd gotten gifts for Mom and Dad. Nothing amazing, some perfume for Mom, and a sweater for my dad, but at least they'd have something tomorrow when I went over for lunch.

I'd also gotten a little something for Lucy, which was why I was so late. She loved to sketch out designs on those huge artists' pads, so I'd picked up half a dozen sketch pads and a set of her favorite drawing pencils. It wasn't much, but I wanted her to know that I'd been thinking about her. I'd never stopped thinking about her.

I was amazed to see that almost every seat in the room was occupied. Most of the people look like they were dressed ready to party, in sparkling frocks and heels, but they were all engrossed, their attention on Lucy, who stood at the front.

I settled in one of the few empty seats at the back.

"This message isn't about stopping you from enjoying yourselves tonight or any night when you want to go out and have a drink." Lucy walked slowly backward and forward as she talked. She had no notecards in her hand or any tablet. She was speaking from the heart.

I was as transfixed as everyone else.

"The decision you make when you get behind the wheel of a car after you've been drinking could be one that affects you forever. And not just you." She lifted something in her hand and pressed it. An enormous picture of Emily flashed up on the screen behind her.

It was like someone had slammed into me from behind. I gripped the back of the chair in front of me, my gaze fixed on the picture. Everything in the room faded away. All I could stare at was Emily's face.

"When you drive drunk, or even if you drive after one or two drinks, your abilities are impaired." Lucy gestured to the picture of Emily. "Your reactions are slower, your vision is disturbed, and your brain processes information at a different rate."

It was like a storm was heading toward me. I saw it but couldn't move. My fingers grew numb, my breath faded, and a stabbing pain lanced through me. I couldn't look away.

Lucy's gaze slid around the room. "The woman you're looking at was my best friend, Emily Danvers. Just over a year ago, she was out, getting last minute Christmas gifts. The driver of the car who hit her had four glasses of red wine at his office Christmas party. He wasn't blind drunk, but his reactions were half the speed they would have been if he'd been sober. He didn't see the red light and slammed into the side of Emily's car at forty miles an hour."

Everyone in the room stilled.

Lucy looked around again, her eyes large and her face pale. "The paramedics arrived on the scene shortly after the accident. They believe she died instantly from massive head trauma."

I couldn't breathe. I couldn't even blink. It all came crashing back to me. Emily was dead. She was gone. I'd never see her again. Neither would Lucy. We'd been holding onto our grief so tightly, thinking it shielded us. All it had done was stop us from living.

"I lost my best friend that day," Lucy said. "Parents lost a child, a brother lost his sister. Our worlds were tipped off their axis because of a single decision another person made."

There were several murmurs in the room.

"There was no malice behind that decision, but it was life changing and devastating." She was silent as she nodded slowly. "I want you all to enjoy yourselves tonight but make sensible decisions about how you get home. Give your keys to someone who isn't drinking, get a cab, walk home with a group of friends, and enjoy looking at the Christmas lights and the decorations in peoples' yards. Don't be the person who ruins other people's lives."

My throat closed up. This was too intense. I slid from the seat and shoved my way out the door, barely seeing where I was going. Hearing Lucy lay her grief out to a room full of strangers in the hope she'd save someone was incredible. She was fighting hard to keep other people safe.

The freezing night air whacked me in the face and froze the tears on my cheeks. I needed to get myself together, needed time to shuffle my emotions back into shape. They were a jumbled mess of hope, fear, anticipation and sadness, and I couldn't get the pieces to slot into place.

I'd always cared for Lucy, but after seeing her just now, my feelings were stronger than ever.

Emily was gone. Emily was dead. I would never see Emily again. But that didn't mean the end of my life. And it didn't mean that Lucy's life would be on hold forever as she battled through her loss.

I wanted to live again, and I wanted Lucy by my side when I did.

I scrubbed my frozen cheeks as fresh tears fell, and I fumbled for my keys.

I'd get myself together then go back in the college, wait for Lucy, and tell her exactly how I felt. And I would invite her over for Christmas. Tomorrow would be the start of something new, fresh, and exciting. My insides shook with a mix of terror and hope.

I didn't see the van as I stepped out. I only heard the screech of tires and felt an intense flare of pain before everything went black.

Chapter 11

Lucy

I put my head between my knees, exhausted and heartsick.

My eyes stung whether they were open or closed. Dawn slowly crept over the rooftops to reach Kelvin's hospital room. Christmas Day. Not quite how I'd planned to spend this morning.

Word of an accident had filtered into the college as I'd finished my talk last night. I hadn't known it was Kelvin who'd been injured until I got a call from his parents.

Why was he even there? Had he gone to hear my talk? How could it be him?

I shook my head. None of that mattered. I stared at his face, willing his eyes to open. Finally.

"Still here, I see."

I twisted to look over my shoulder. The doctor had snuck in on silent sneakers. "I didn't want him to wake up and be alone. His parents have stepped out for a few minutes to make some calls to family and friends."

He nodded, his attention on the records.

"Any signs of improvement?" I asked the same question every time a doctor or nurse came in the room.

"Everything is stable, which is a positive sign. We have to be careful with head injuries, though. The brain is a delicate organ. The body will often temporarily shut down while it deals with trauma. His lack of consciousness shouldn't alarm you."

But it did. Kelvin had fractured his leg and arm, but the doctors were most worried about the injury to his head.

"He's got everything on his side," the doctor said. "He's young and healthy. He'll wake up soon. I know that is little comfort to you right now, but you need to stay strong for him."

"Of course." I reached to smooth the hair back from his forehead. "I can't imagine life without him." My chest had begun to fill with a cold empty ache with every hour he remained in that bed and didn't move.

"He'll wake up soon. All signs point to a positive outcome." The doctor did several more checks before nodding at me and leaving the room.

I wrapped my fingers around Kelvin's hand. "If there is such a thing as magic at Christmas, then you'll wake up right now. You'll make a full recovery, and everything will be good again. Please come back to me, Kelvin." I leaned forward and kissed his cheek.

His eyes remained shut.

Hurried footsteps approached the door, and Kelvin's mom and dad appeared and walked through the doorway.

"We just saw the doctor leave. Any change?" His mom walked over and squeezed my shoulder, her gaze on her son.

"No. The doctor checked how things were doing. He sounded positive." I forced myself to seem calm, even though my insides raged like an out-of-control bush fire.

"That's good." Mrs. Danvers glanced at her husband. "Don't you think?"

He simply nodded. He'd barely spoken more than a dozen words, his face stern and tight.

I vacated the chair, so Mrs. Danvers could sit, and rubbed the small of my back.

"Why don't you take a walk outside?" Mrs. Danvers said. "Some fresh air will do you good."

"I don't want to leave Kelvin," I said.

She nodded before taking hold of his hand. "I understand. We've just called around the rest of the family, so they know what's going on. I hated doing it. It felt like we were ruining everyone's Christmas Day, but I wanted them to know."

"Of course." I glanced at Kelvin's dad. He looked like he was asleep on his feet as he swayed from side to side, dark shadows under his eyes and a rare thatch of stubble on his chin.

I walked over and took hold of his elbow. "How are you doing, Mr. Danvers?"

His eyes snapped open, and he blinked at me blearily. "I've been better, love. I can't stop thinking about Emily and what happened."

"Stop with that talk. This is nothing like that," Mrs. Danvers said, her voice high in pitch. "Kelvin's been injured, but he'll be fine. We'll have him home in a few days and can celebrate Christmas then."

My throat clogged with a cascade of tears I'd been holding onto, but I forced them down with a swallow. Getting tearful and upset wouldn't do any good.

"Although this is a horrible way for us to re-connect, Lucy, I'm glad you're here," Mrs. Danvers said.

"Me, too," I said. "I'm sorry. I shouldn't have stayed away so long. But I... well, it seemed easier."

"We understand. Confronting the memories of Emily is hard. I remember how much she loved you. She was always talking about you and the plans you made together. She cherished your friendship."

I nodded, not sure I was able to speak.

"You were a good friend to her," Mr. Danvers said, his voice gruff.

"I tried to be," I said. "Thanks for the things you sent over from her apartment. I'll treasure them."

"Of course. You're welcome." Mrs. Danvers smiled. "I hear you found Emily's cat."

"Yes, of course. I should have thought to tell you about Fenella," I said.

"Kelvin told me. It's astonishing. Emily would be thrilled to know you're looking after her," Mrs. Danvers said.

"Fenella's a little quieter than I remember her when she lived with Emily, but she's coming out of herself. I think she's finally making herself at home in my apartment," I said. "I'm glad to have the company, actually. The place doesn't feel so empty now I have her."

"Emily always said a house wasn't a home unless it had at least one cat." Mrs. Danvers' smile appeared wistful.

"She'd have had a dozen cats if she could afford them," Mr. Danvers said.

"She always had 'rescue kitten' on the top of her Christmas list every year." Mrs. Danvers sat up straight, her forehead wrinkling. "You sound as if you've not got anyone special in your life, Lucy."

I looked at Kelvin. "No. I'm on my own."

"No one should be on their own at Christmas," Mrs. Danvers said. "You must come and spend some time with us if you're not going to see your family."

That sweet offer had tears springing in my eyes. "That's generous of you, but you're going to be busy. Kelvin will need looking after when he wakes."

"I can look after my son and have you over for lunch," Mrs. Danvers said. "And I know he'll hate me fussing over him. You'll be a welcome distraction. And Kelvin mentioned you when we spoke on the phone just before his accident. I suggested we invite you over for Christmas, so it's no bother."

"There's not going to be much of a Christmas now." Mr. Danvers rubbed the back of his neck.

"There will be if Lucy is coming." Mrs. Danvers tilted her chin. There appeared to be desperation glinting in her eyes as her gaze met mine.

"Of course. I'd love to visit." I couldn't get out of this, and I wasn't sure I wanted to.

I tightened my grip on Mr. Danvers' arm, feeling his body shake. The guy must be running on empty, fueled by nothing but his desire for his son to wake up.

I grabbed another seat and set it by Kelvin's bed, before easing Mr Danvers into it.

"Thanks, love." He patted my hand.

"I'll go get us coffee and maybe something to eat if anyone is hungry," I said.

"I'm not sure I could eat," Mrs. Danvers said. "But I'd appreciate a coffee."

"I'll be right back." I'd just reached the door, when a gasp from Mrs. Danvers had me turning. "What is it?"

She was leaning over Kelvin. "His eyes moved."

I raced back to the bed, and the three of us stood there, staring down at him.

Kelvin groaned and shifted, his face wrinkling into a mask of pain.

"Kelvin, can you hear me?" his mom said. "You're in the hospital. You're okay. Everyone's here. Your dad's here, and Lucy's here, too."

His eyes inched open, and his tongue slid across his lips.

My heart thundered so loudly, I imagined every patient in the hospital could hear it.

Kelvin's gaze flicked to me before looking away. Then it shot back, and his eyes opened fully.

"Yes! You see, Lucy's here." His mom's voice was choked as she looked down at him, tears on her cheeks, and a huge smile on her face. "Lucy, say something to him."

I coughed to ease the lump in my throat. "Kelvin, can you hear your mom?"

He nodded his head a fraction. "What happened?"

Everyone sighed at the same time.

"You don't remember?" Mrs. Danvers said. "You were outside Trenton College. You got hit by a van."

"A van?" He cleared his throat. "Any chance of some water?"

"Of course." His mom passed him a cup with a straw, which he drank out of.

"That's better." His voice sounded stronger. "I got hit?"

"We're not exactly sure what happened," his mom said. "The man driving the van said you simply stepped out in front of him. It doesn't matter now. We're just glad you're awake. How do you feel?"

His gaze returned to me. My heart stuttered in my chest, a flare of tangled emotions shooting through me, making my brain buzz, my stomach clench, and my toes tingle.

"I really do feel like I've been hit by a van," Kelvin said.

We all laughed, and some of the achingly strong tension in the room faded.

"Go get the doctor," Mrs. Danvers said to her husband.

He nodded, patted Kelvin's hand, and dashed out of the room.

I couldn't stop looking at Kelvin, and he seemed to be struggling with the same problem. It would only be a matter of time before his mom noticed there was something going on between us. But what was going on? The way my pulse slammed in my veins, I needed to find out.

The next five minutes were a flurry of activity as the doctor arrived and checked Kelvin over.

"Everything's looking good," he said. "We'll run some scans to be on the safe side, but the best thing now will be bedrest."

The coil of tension inside me unwound. With an almost Herculean effort, I tore my gaze from Kelvin and stepped back from the bed, even though

I wanted to throw myself into his arms and never let go. "I expect you want some time on your own."

"Actually, Mom, Dad, can you give me a few minutes with Lucy?" Kelvin shifted up in the bed. "There's something we need to talk about."

Mrs. Danvers' expression moved from concerned to smiley. "Oh! Of course. I need to talk to the doctor, anyway."

"Thanks, Mom."

"Let's go get some coffee," she said to her husband.

"We've only just gotten back," Mr. Danvers said. "We should sit with Kelvin a while."

"We will. Let's leave these two on their own for now." She took hold of her husband's hand and guided him out of the room. She smiled broadly at me before nodding at Kelvin.

I repressed a grin. Moms always knew when something was going on.

My heart felt like it would burst out of my chest, and I found it hard to look Kelvin in the eye.

"I heard your talk," he said softly.

I licked my suddenly dry lips and nodded.

"I couldn't stop thinking about you. I hated the thought of you being on your own on Christmas Eve. I wanted to see you. And then, well, I saw that picture of Emily on the screen, and—"

"Oh, Kelvin! Of course." I grabbed his uninjured hand between mine. "If I'd have known you were coming, I'd have warned you that I used pictures of Emily. You don't mind?"

"Of course not. If other people hearing what happened to my sister makes them stop before they get behind the wheel, then it's helping others. I don't know how you do it, though. How you can talk about it so calmly?"

"My insides are anything but calm when I give that talk. I've spoken publicly a dozen times about that night. It never gets any easier."

His thumb brushed across my knuckles, sending a thrill of pleasure through my arm. "You're incredible. The bravest person I've ever met."

I let out a shuddering sigh. "Except when I'm hiding from the world the rest of the time. That's all I've been doing this past year, literally refusing to leave my apartment. Pretending I'm so busy with work that I don't have time for anything else. My life's been on pause since Emily died. I did it because I thought I was keeping myself safe, stopping myself from getting attached to anyone for fear of losing them. All I lost was a year of my life."

His fingers tightened around my hand, and he tugged me closer to the bed. "Same here. I've been so angry with everyone and everything since Emily died. I was convinced I'd failed her. Certain I could have changed things, if only I'd been a better brother."

"You know that's not—"

"True? Deep down, I do, but that doesn't make it any easier. I was supposed to look out for her. I felt like a failure. I buried my head in work and refused to talk about the rage inside me. I trapped it, thinking it would go, but it remained, simmering away and occasionally exploding at the wrong people."

"You can't help how you feel," I said. "You had a right to be angry. But not at yourself."

"Maybe I could have made it easier on myself if I shared how I felt. I shut down. I refused to let anybody in because I was so worried I'd fail them, too." His gaze met mine, and he held it. "Lucy, the thought of losing you makes me sick. We've known each other most of our lives. I didn't realize how much I missed you when you disappeared. You were always there. And then you weren't. That hurt almost as much as losing Emily."

"I shouldn't have shut you out," I said. "You or your family. We could have helped each other heal. Maybe it wouldn't have been so painful if we'd have been together."

"It would still have hurt like a dozen angry hornets stabbing at my heart, but maybe you're right," he said. "I should have talked more about Emily. I loved sharing those memories of her with you. It did me good. I already feel less angry. You make me less angry. When I'm with you, I feel amazing."

His declaration made my insides melt. "Even after just being hit by a van?"

He snorted a quiet laugh. "Even then."

I held his hand against my chest. "And I feel less afraid to face the world. You helped me do that. Finding Fenella at Forever Paws was the first step, I think. I stumbled into that place not knowing what I needed but desperate for a shred of comfort. Everything seemed so bleak. I don't know what it was that day, coincidence, fate, or Christmas magic that led me to Fenella, but it was a tiny spark of possibility to cling to. A flicker of hope that life may get better. Then you showed up at my apartment, and the flame grew. I started to feel again. For so long, I had this blankness inside me."

"I'm helping take that away?" The concern and sincerity in his voice had me blinking away tears.

I smiled down at him. "You are. You and that funny little fur ball have made my heart beat again. Until you came back into my life, I couldn't remember the last time I smiled. You make me want to smile all the time."

"Now I've found you again, I don't want to let you go," Kelvin said. "We deserve happiness. I convinced myself I wasn't worthy of it because of what happened to Emily. Because I hadn't been able to keep her safe, I needed to suffer."

My heart hurt hearing those words. Kelvin was such a decent man. He didn't deserve to agonize over something he couldn't control.

He smiled. "I feel differently now. If you let me stay in your life, I promise I'll work hard to make sure you laugh every day. I want to be a part of your life for a very long time. Forever, if you'll have me."

I swiped away a tear and leaned over the bed. "Of course, I'll have you. I've had a crush on you ever since we were kids."

"Yeah, I sort of knew that." He grinned at me.

My mouth fell open, and my cheeks flamed. "You did?"

"Sure. I mean, look at me."

I choked out a laugh. "Bashed up, with two fractured limbs and stuck in the hospital over Christmas. You're every girl's dream."

"There's only one girl's dream I want to be." His smile faded, and he cupped my face with his uninjured hand.

His tender admission made my heart fold. I leaned closer, my eyes closing.

Kelvin's kiss was just a feather touch to start with. Then it intensified, and I found myself pressed against his chest, my hands on his face, my breath ragged and cheeks on fire.

He pulled back. "You're the best Christmas gift I've ever received. Finding you again, having you back in my life, it's changed everything."

I rested my forehead against him and drank him in. Sure, he was bashed up from the accident, but he was my Kelvin. Being with him was like coming home. His family embraced me with a warm, all-encompassing love, and he'd do the same now I'd finally opened my heart to him.

"We'll always love Emily," I said. "But I can guarantee, she'd have kicked our behinds for not getting on with our lives."

"She absolutely would." Kelvin kissed my cheek softly. "So, let's not hide anymore. There'll always be the possibility of loss, but without that risk, we won't experience love or discover how amazing our lives can be together."

There was a knock on the door, and I stepped away from the bed when I saw Kelvin's parents returning.

"Have you had a chance to talk?" Mrs. Danvers raised her eyebrows and smiled at me.

I pressed my fingers to my hot cheeks, not able to stop grinning. "I think we've said everything we need to say."

"For now." Kelvin winked at me. "We're going to do a lot more talking when I'm back on my feet."

Mrs. Danvers passed me a coffee. "I need to discuss our Christmas plans. We're going to have to postpone things for a few days until you get out of the hospital, Kelvin."

"You never know, they may discharge me today," he said. "I haven't felt this great in a long time."

"There's not a chance of that," Mr. Danvers said. "We spoke to the doctor. You're in for at least another forty-eight hours."

Mrs. Danvers sat on the chair next to Kelvin's bed. "Once you're out of here, we'll have a real family celebration. All of us." She reached over, took my hand, and squeezed it.

"I'd really love that," I said.

"And you must bring Fenella," Mrs. Danvers said. "Emily always brought her over on the holidays. I loved spoiling that little cutie. I've missed her. Almost as much as I've missed not seeing you, Lucy."

"Of course. I've missed you all, too." I checked the time. "I need to head back to my apartment and feed Fenella. She's been on her own for hours. She must be wondering what's going on."

"Don't be long," Kelvin said.

"You just try to keep me away." I grinned at Kelvin before nodding goodbye to his parents and practically skipping out of the room and along the corridor of the hospital.

Everywhere I looked, I saw flashes of tinsel, sparkling trees, and happy faces on this most joyful of Christmas mornings.

Now I'd opened my eyes and stopped hiding from the world, I was experiencing the warmth, love, and joy that happened at this most magical time of the year.

And it was magic. Christmas was a time of wishes, finding hope, and giving thanks for everything I had in my life.

I didn't have Emily anymore, but I had my happy memories of her. And I had so much to look forward to. Christmas was all about new beginnings and happiness, and I was finally ready to let it into my life.

Epilogue 1 – one year later

Lucy

A light sprinkling of snow covered the cemetery ground as I crouched in front of Emily's grave and laid a large Christmas wreath on it. My eyes were full of tears, and there was a soft ache in my heart as I stood and stepped back into Kelvin's warm, solid embrace.

We stood in silence for several minutes, both of us lost in our thoughts about Emily.

"It doesn't seem like two years since she's been gone," Kelvin said.

"It really doesn't," I said. "She's still alive in my head and my heart." I rested my hand on the top of the cat travel pram. It seemed only right that I bring Fenella when we visited Emily.

Kelvin squeezed me tightly, his warmth radiating into me and keeping out the winter chill. We'd been almost inseparable over the last year, getting to know each other all over again, building a life that was intricately entangled. It was, at times, terrifying and exhilarating. The risk of opening my heart to him had been absolutely worth it.

Fenella scratched the cover of her cat pram and meowed loudly.

"You think she wants to get out?" Kelvin asked. "She's such a fair weather cat. She won't last ten seconds in this cold."

"Normally, she hates the snow," I said. "If ever I open the apartment door for her to go outside, if there's snow on the ground, she turns her nose up and walks away."

Her persistent meowing continued.

I bent and unzipped the edge of the pram cover. "What's the matter with you?"

Fenella's nose poked out, and it instantly wrinkled.

I grinned. "Yes, it's snowing. I know how precious you are about your fur." Fenella had been an absolute delight since I'd added her to my life. It had taken her a month before she'd shaken off the sadness that covered her. Now, she loved nothing more than playing, long grooming sessions, and snuggling on my lap while I worked at my desk. She brought joy into my heart, adding to the huge scoop Kelvin provided on a daily basis.

A paw poked out the hole, and she shoved the zip down.

"She's really keen on getting out," Kelvin said. "You should let her. She won't go far. Not in this weather."

I shrugged and stood back. "The snowy ground is all yours, Fenella."

Fenella hopped out of the pram. She picked up one front paw then set it down before doing the same with the other one and shaking off the snow. She looked around, and her blue eyes narrowed.

"She's going to get right back in that pram any second," I said.

Instead of doing that, Fenella walked to Emily's headstone and stared at it, as if reading the inscription.

My eyes widened. "You don't think she knows this is Emily's final resting place?"

"Of course she doesn't," Kelvin said. "Fenella's smart, but she's just a cat."

Fenella glanced at him and hissed quietly.

I laughed in surprise at her sass. "She disagrees with that comment." I stared in wonder as Fenella walked around the headstone, rubbing against it and flicking her tail.

"Will you look at that?" Kelvin shook his head. "She really does seem to know this place is important."

"That cat's a lot smarter than you give her credit for," I said. "I'm certain she's never forgotten Emily and how much they loved each other."

My heart gave a little stutter as Fenella placed her front paws on the headstone and pressed her nose against it.

"Maybe this has something to do with that Christmas magic you believe in." Kelvin wrapped his arm around my waist.

"You believe in it, too. After all, it helped us find each other when we were lost."

"More like my mom reconnected us when she made me bring a box of Emily's things to your apartment."

"Mom magic or Christmas magic, they're both powerful forces and to be respected at all times."

He chuckled. "It's almost as if Fenella's wishing Emily a Merry Christmas."

"You could be right," I said. "Hey, have we got time to stop at Forever Paws on our way home? I want to drop off that picture of us to go on their wall of joy. And the donation."

"Of course. It'll be good to see the place. And I meant to tell you, they wrote to Mom and Dad last week. They've erected two new cat pens with the legacy Emily left them in her will. They'll be able to take in more cats, thanks to her."

I smiled. "Emily will be remembered forever."

"Neither of us will ever forget her." Kelvin reached over and opened the locket around my neck. Inside was the same picture of Emily, but there was a picture of him, as well. The two people I loved more than anything in the world were right by my heart.

He kissed the locket then placed it against my skin before snuggling my thick scarf around my neck.

I stepped forward and touch the headstone. "Have a great Christmas, Emily. We'll be thinking about you."

Fenella rubbed around the stone another couple of times. Then she weaved around my legs, rubbed against Kelvin, and hopped back in the pram.

We all said our goodbyes and headed to the car as the snow fell faster.

My life changed forever after I lost Emily, but that didn't mean it had to end. I'd rediscovered joy and a happiness I thought wasn't possible.

Kelvin smiled at me once I'd settled Fenella securely in the back of the car. "Are we ready for a joyful Christmas?"

I grinned at him and took hold of his hand. "So long as I'm with you and Fenella, it'll be amazing."

He leaned over and kissed me. "I couldn't agree more."

Fenella meowed from the back seat.

Kelvin chuckled. "And yes, I include you in that. Even though you're always chewing on my sweaters and making holes in them. That cat is freakily obsessed with wool."

I smiled, feeling like a warm, comforting blanket of love surrounded me as we headed away from the cemetery.

I'd found joy at Christmas again, and it was all thanks to Kelvin and Fenella.

And maybe just a little Christmas magic, too.

Epilogue 2

♥

Fenella

"Have you got room for one more piece of turkey?" Mrs. Danvers dangled a delicious treat in front of me.

"Any more food and that cat will get mistaken for the Christmas pudding," Mr. Danvers said from his easy chair in the living room.

I ignored that rude comment and took the succulent piece of meat as delicately as possible, despite the urge to snap it out of Mrs. Danvers' fingers and gobble it in a single bite. She made amazing turkey.

That was one thing I didn't miss about Emily. She was a terrible cook. She always used to overcook my fresh salmon. And as for the one occasion when she cooked a pot roast, I still cringe when I remember the smoke alarm screeching its distress as it saw the charred meat. Such a tragic loss.

I finished my turkey and scampered past Mr. Danvers. I remembered this place. I used to come here with Emily before she disappeared. Well, I know now that she didn't disappear. She never left me. She didn't have a choice but to go.

Lucy and Kelvin had talked about Emily a lot over the last year. And although I still got a flutter in my stomach that was a bit like hunger when I remembered Emily was gone, I knew she didn't abandon me. She never stopped loving me.

My nose wrinkled at a sound that had become all too familiar in my everyday life. Kelvin and Lucy were kissing under a bright green sprig of something with white berries on it. They did that a lot. The kissing, not the making out under festive foliage. The noise sometimes woke me up.

They were both happy now. They laughed a lot as well as kissed. They were different from last Christmas. In a good way.

Another amazing thing that was different was the amount of turkey I'd been fed today. Turkey was a close second to chicken, and I took all the scraps I could get. I only got a taste of this delicious bird once or twice a year, so I made the most of it. And it got cold in winter, so an extra layer of internal insulation was important. No one liked getting chilly paws.

I headed into the family room and looked around. Great, I had the place to myself.

I'd been spending a lot of time in here since I'd arrived on Christmas Eve. There were lots of pictures of Emily placed around the room. Ones of her when she was small, before we met. Then pictures of her when she was bigger. There was one of her wearing a funny flat board on her head and a long black gown. Lucy was also in that picture, wearing the same clothes. They were grinning at each other.

I hopped onto the mantelpiece with a natural grace that befitted me and rubbed my face against my favorite picture. I was in it with Emily. She was holding me up, and we were looking straight at the camera. My adorable pink tongue stuck out, and Emily was mimicking me. She must have known I'd only done that because it made her laugh.

I would always love my first human the most. There would always be a place in my heart for Emily. But I also knew a cat's life was meant to be full of joy, cuddles, and being treated like a queen.

And I had a purpose now. I'd been waiting at Forever Paws for my new special someone. Emily had made sure I'd find Lucy, so I could watch over her. Emily would want me to make sure her friends and family were safe and happy. So, that's what I did. And I'd been doing a great job for the last year.

I'd taught Lucy the best way to groom me, the kind of food I liked to eat, and the exact brand of litter I needed in my tray. I also got her to laugh a lot. Although maybe not as often as Kelvin did. Lucy always smiled when he was around.

There were plenty of times when Lucy got things wrong, but Emily had shown me that kindness and patience were how you treated someone when they were slow on the uptake.

Lucy tried her best, so I didn't leave too many furballs in her shoes or chew through all her sweaters, no matter how yummy that wool was.

"There you are." Lucy appeared in the doorway, a small wrapped gift in her hands. "It's time to open our presents. I got you something special."

I trotted over as she knelt on the floor and held out the gift. I knew exactly what to do with this. I grabbed it in my teeth and shook it before tearing off the wrapping with my claws. I was hoping it would be the deluxe catnip I'd seen on the screen when Lucy had been browsing for my Christmas gifts, but it didn't smell like catnip.

Something pink and sparkly fell out of the wrapping. Nope, that wasn't catnip.

Lucy picked it up and held it out for me to sniff. It was curved with a small gold heart on it. "We've got matching lockets. Yours even opens."

I looked at the locket as she opened it. Inside, there was a tiny picture of Emily and me together, and on the other side a miniature picture of Lucy and Kelvin.

I approved. I always liked anything pink. Emily used to tell me it was my favorite color. She was always right about important things like that.

I resisted the urge to back away as Lucy clipped the collar around my neck and adjusted it till it was a snug fit.

"Now you have us all close to your heart, just where we belong." She kissed the top of my head. "Let's join everyone, so we can open our presents together and find out what else Santa has brought you. He's been very generous this year."

My ears pricked, and my tail quivered. Would I find a drinking fountain under the tree? That was on the top of my Christmas wish list.

I allowed Lucy to scoop me into her arms and snuggle me against her chest, giving a quiet purr of acceptance as I rested against her warm, soft sweater.

I'd never forget Emily, but I had a happy life. It involved lots of cuddles, great food, and a warm, soft bed. Plus, I had my memories of Emily. If ever I got sad or confused about what had happened to her, I thought about those happier times.

Emily would approve of all this. From my new collar to the way her mom and dad smiled again and made plans for the future. She'd probably even be happy about all the smoochy noises Kelvin and Lucy made. I was still undecided about those noises, but they did make Lucy happy, so I shouldn't complain.

Lucy sat next to Kelvin and kissed his cheek.

I snuggled in her lap and sucked on the edge of her sweater before sending my own little cat kiss to Emily.

Merry Christmas, Emily. And Merry Christmas to my amazing new family.

About Author

Karen Drew loves romance, gentle heroes who never give up on true love, and animals. Sweet romance, quirky pets, and happily ever afters fill her books.

When she's not writing, she's exploring the world of interesting flavors of tea, enjoying cake, and dreaming of new happily ever afters to delight readers.

Join her on Facebook for regular tea and cake updates, book news, and regular chats about all things animal:
www.facebook.com/karendrewauthor

Or join her newsletter and receive a **free** book:
https://BookHip.com/ZKJQFF

Also By

♥

12 Cats
Merry Christmas, Kitten
Joy to the Cats
Mistletoe and Meows

Furs Hill sweet romance
Love, Furballs, and Forever
Love, Pawprints, and Promises
Love, Happiness, and Hounds
Love, Kittens, and Kisses

If you enjoyed

Joy to the Cats

turn the page to read an extract from the next 12
Cats of Christmas Romance

MISTLETOE AND MEOWS
ISBN: 978-1-915378-23-1

Chapter 1

Gabe

"You look like a jerk dressed as a Christmas elf. Aren't you too old to play dress up?" Ernie snatched the wrapped gift away from me and scowled at it as if it might explode in his hand.

"Happy Christmas to you too, buddy," I said.

Ernie's frown deepened, and he shook the box. He didn't have much to smile about, having to spend Christmas in a shelter for the homeless.

I patted him on the arm. It was only a small gesture of kindness, just like the gift.

"It had better not be socks. All the so called good samaritans keep turning up with socks. How many feet do they think I have?"

"It gets cold out. Socks are a great gift. And you need to keep warm. It's been below freezing these last few nights. I reckon we'll get new snow fall before Christmas Day." I adjusted my pointed ears.

Ernie grunted. "I'll take a bottle of whiskey if you've got any in that sack of yours. That'll keep the chill out."

I chuckled as I sorted through the gifts. "No alcohol. Besides, you're on a winning streak. How long has it been?"

"Six months, two weeks, three days," Ernie checked his battered watch, "and twelve hours."

"You'll soon be getting your one-year sober token."

"And I'll celebrate with a glass of water. Whoopee do-dah!"

"Enjoy your socks, Ernie." I hoisted the sack over my shoulder and headed to the next gift deposit site.

Pete and Archie were ahead of me, singing out of tune Christmas songs as they carried their loaded sacks of donated presents.

I rounded the corner and spotted half a dozen regulars waiting for our arrival. They all knew the drill and where to find us if they wanted clean socks, warm hats, and other practical things to keep them going at this harsh time of year.

A group of us volunteered to do the Christmas gift drop off for the street homeless every December in Silver Birch. I made the trip back home especially for this. But this year was different. This year, I wasn't planning on leaving.

A curvy woman dressed in a long red coat, a hat with a bobble pulled down over her ears, walked toward the group, pushing a bright pink pram with silver tinsel wrapped around the handles. She stopped and spoke to the homeless guys.

I raised an eyebrow. Most women on their own would cross the road and avoid them, thinking they could get in trouble.

Several of them looked in the pram, smiles on their weather-beaten faces. Two of the guys laughed and nudged each other.

I frowned at their response. Why were they laughing at the baby?

Archie and Pete's arrival distracted the group, and they left the woman alone and headed over to receive their Christmas gifts.

The woman stood watching the gifts get handed out for a few seconds, a smile on her face.

I walked over to her and tilted my head. There was something familiar about that cute button nose and those plump cheeks that were bright pink from the biting cold.

"Hey! I don't think you need anything from our Christmas sacks, do you?" I said.

She glanced my way. Her flushed cheeks grew even pinker and her large, dark eyes widened. "Oh! No, I don't need help. I'm not homeless." She looked down at her coat. "Do I look homeless to you?"

"Nope. You look great. I'm Gabe." I nodded, grinning as I took in her poker straight blonde hair sticking out from under the hat, curves in all the right places, and those deep, mysterious eyes. And those lips. They were possibly the most kissable I'd ever seen.

She simply nodded, not giving out her name.

Okay, mysterious lady, you can be coy. Coy and seriously cute.

"I've been doing the Christmas homeless present drop for five years. I come back every year to help at St. Peter's Church," I said.

Her full lips pursed. "That's good of you. Not many people are charitable to those who find themselves on the street. I feel sorry for them. My toes go numb just imagining sleeping rough."

"Yeah, these guys rarely get many people looking out for them."

She nodded. "I know. I often stop when I'm on my walks to see how they're doing. I help when I can, but sometimes, all they seem to want is a kind word and for someone to notice them. It can make their day."

"I bet it does. Do you live around here?" This was getting interesting. How had I missed this gorgeous woman on my previous visits home?

Those almond eyes narrowed a fraction. "I've lived here all my life."

Her tone suggested I should know that, but I still couldn't place that face. "Me, too. Well, I've been away for a while, but I'm moving back if everything pans out."

"Lucky town."

Was that a hint of sarcasm beneath the sweetness? "It sure is. Maybe you could show me around to make me see what I've been missing."

"Oh, no, that won't work. I'm too busy to do that." She adjusted her grip on the pram and gave the tinsel a tweak with her gloved hand.

"Busy with your baby? How old?"

She bit her bottom lip, drawing my attention back to that full mouth. "Nine, twelve, and fifteen."

My eyebrows shot up. She was way too young to have children that age. "I meant the baby in the pram."

She lifted one shoulder, a defiant tilt to her chin. "They're all my babies, no matter how old they are."

I leaned closer and peered through the mesh netting. Three pairs of brilliant green eyes blinked back at me.

I jerked away, almost falling as my legs hit the bag of gifts I'd dropped. "You've got cats in that pram!"

A shiver of a smile crossed her face. "They can't be outside when it's this cold." She rested a hand on top of the pram cover, as if gently warning me not to get too close.

"Why are you pushing around three cats?" I looked back in at the cats. They were snuggled on a soft gray blanket. They looked content.

She let out a soft huff, and it clouded around her in the chilly air. "They have particular needs. Animals need help as well as people. You help the homeless, and I help the cats."

"Oh! Sure. I like cats. Is there something wrong with them? Is that why they have to be in a pram?"

"The only thing that's wrong with them is the way people have treated them."

I lifted a hand, seeing the fire in her eyes. "I get it. Sometimes, people don't have the sense they were born with. They can't walk?"

The anger in her pretty eyes faded a fraction. "Ginger only has three legs. He lost one after being attacked by a dog. If he walks too much, his back leg is at risk of dislocation, which leaves him in agony. Fluffball has arthritis, so it's painful for her to walk, but she likes to get outside. And Donut has a brain injury, so he can't walk in a straight line. It's too risky to let him free roam."

I whistled out a note. "That's quite a commitment, taking on three cats with special needs."

"I have six. Three of the cats stay at home. They have a large outdoor run, so get plenty of fresh air and exercise."

Oh, boy! I'd just found myself a pretty, crazy cat lady. I was smart enough to know not to tangle with a woman and her cats, but this woman was drawing me in.

I needed to know more about her. "They must keep you busy."

"Which is why I don't have time to show you around town. If you'll excuse me, I need to get home. I can't have my babies getting cold." She pushed the pram in front of her, her gaze fixed forward, her chin up.

I grabbed the sack of gifts and left it with Pete, before hurrying to catch up and walk beside her.

There was something special about this cat lady. Maybe it was the fire in her belly or her fierce protectiveness over something she loved. And her cute face was an added bonus.

She shot me a cautious glance as I caught up with her. "Are you going my way?"

"I need to grab something from my car. It's just up ahead. If you don't mind, I'll walk with you."

She gave another little shrug.

I couldn't resist sneaking a few glances at her as we walked. Those apple cheeks, wide mouth, and big dark eyes made her physically my type. But I wasn't just interested in looks. Sure, being attracted to your other half was important, but I needed to know the woman I was with was honest and straightforward. I'd been played around with before, and there was no way it was happening again.

She cleared her throat. "Um... what brings you back to Silver Birch?"

"Oh, you know, life. Things changing. New beginnings." I waved a hand in the air, not quite ready to lay everything out for her just yet. We all had pasts. Some of them messier than others.

"Well, welcome home. I'd never want to live anywhere else. I love it here."

"Small town life sure takes some beating. Do you have family here?"

"Don't we all?"

That wasn't an answer, more a side-step. "Sure. I mean, do your parents live around here?"

"Where's your car?"

"It's right there." I pointed at my new sleek black Audi, but I hadn't missed her avoiding my question again. Maybe she didn't get along with her parents. After all, you couldn't pick the family you were born into. There may be problems she didn't like to talk about. But I'd circle back to that when I got a moment.

And I planned to have more moments with this gorgeous woman. "Hey, you never told me your name."

She stopped the pink pram beside my car. Our gazes locked, and my pulse raced. She was a shot of sugar straight in the veins, making me feel like smiling for no reason.

"Is that important?"

"It will be the next time I bump into you. I've already told you my name. It's Gabe. Gabe Blackwell. And you are..."

She gave a swift nod. "Rhyannon."

"Just Rhyannon, like the singer?"

"For now." Her gaze ran over my car.

I placed a protective hand on it, just as she'd done with her cats. I'd only bought the car last week. It was a treat after securing the contract to refit the old Brewer's office block downtown. That money would see me right for years, give me a chance to put down roots, and find a place to call my own.

And I wanted to do that with someone. Maybe even someone like Rhyannon if she opened up a little and let me learn more about her.

"Do you like the car?" I said.

"So long as whatever I drive gets me from A to B, that's all I care about." Her gaze swept over the car again. It looked like her judgment of my new ride wasn't positive.

"Cars aren't for everyone. What kind of things do you like to do in your spare time?" I wanted to see what we had in common, and help bring down those walls Rhyannon had up.

Her fingers flexed around the pram handles. "I need to get these little ones inside and in the warm. We'll be late for their dinner if I don't hurry."

That was another side-step. Why all the mystery? "You're a real Christmas angel to unwanted cats."

A brief smile revealed two cute dimples, and my heart stuttered a beat.

"You could be too if you wanted to be. Unwanted animals always need protecting."

"I could. And I love animals. But how would that work?"

Rhyannon fumbled in her purse and handed me a card. "Meet me here tomorrow evening at six o'clock. That's where the Christmas magic happens for the cats."

I stared at the card. Forever Paws animal shelter. That name was familiar.

I lifted my head as she walked away. "Wait! Do you need a ride anywhere?"

"No, I've not got far to go." She glanced over her shoulder. "And don't you have elf duties?"

I cast a regretful look at the bag of gifts I'd left with Pete. I couldn't abandon what I was doing, no matter how cute this woman was. "What will we be doing at Forever Paws?"

"Helping those who need it the most, just as you do for the homeless. Enjoy your evening, Mr. Blackwell."

I would. I got satisfaction from giving back. And I also enjoyed watching Rhyannon walk away. I loved a curvy woman. And this one had fire in her as well as sweet dimples.

I looked back at the card and my grin widened. Had she just asked me out, or was this business?

I pulled out my phone and called Chris. "Guess what, buddy. I've found another mission that needs my attention. This one comes covered in fur."

There was something about this woman that intrigued me. And with some Christmas luck, I'd figure out just how amazing she was.

Joy to the Cats is available in paperback and ebook format.
ISBN: 978-1-915378-23-1